"I Know You're A Player— Different Woman Every Night Kind Of Guy—"

"Hey—" Griffin started to argue, but what the hell could he say? He *was* that guy. At least, he *had* been until he'd made the decision to grow the hell up. For all the good that was doing him.

"No offense," she said quickly. "In this case, your inability to commit is a plus."

"My—"

"Seriously, you're not interested in forever, and trust me when I say I'm not either, Griffin. I just want one good night. A damn fling. And you are s-o-o-o flingable."

Griffin could only stare at her. This was the weirdest situation he'd ever been in. He'd never had a woman come to him with an offer like this one. He'd always been the pursuer not the pursued and frankly, he was a hell of a lot more comfortable when he was calling the shots.

Still, he thought, there was something to be said for variety, right?

Dear Reader,

Every once in a while, when you're writing a book, a secondary character comes across as so vivid, so much fun, you just know you're going to have to tell a story especially *for* that character.

After my book *King's Million-Dollar Secret* was released, I received a lot of letters from readers telling me that they wanted my heroine's best friend, Nicole Baxter, to have her own hero—preferably a King.

It was great knowing that Nicole had won over not only me, but my readers, as well.

Nicole and Griffin King are thrown together when they suddenly become next-door neighbors. Griffin's made it a point to avoid getting involved with single mothers...but Nicole is hard to ignore. Especially when she comes to him with an offer—one spectacular night together, no strings attached.

One night just isn't enough, though, and before he knows it, Griffin is drawn into the circle of the little family and isn't sure he wants to find a way back out.

I really hope you enjoy Nicole's story as much as I did!

I'd love to hear from you. Visit my website at www.maureenchild.com.

Happy reading!

Maureen

The King Next Door

MAUREEN CHILD

First published in Great Britain 2013
by Mills & Boon, an imprint of Harlequin (UK) Limited.
Large Print edition 2013
Harlequin (UK) Limited,
Eton House, 18-24 Paradise Road,
Richmond, Surrey TW9 1SR

© Maureen Child 2013

ISBN: 978 0 263 23787 0

Harlequin (UK) policy is to use papers that are natural,
renewable and recyclable products and made from
wood grown in sustainable forests. The logging
and manufacturing process conform to the legal
environmental regulations of the country of origin.

Printed and bound in Great Britain
by CPI Antony Rowe, Chippenham, Wiltshire

MAUREEN CHILD

writes for Mills & Boon Desire and can't imagine a better job. Being able to indulge your love for romance as well as being able to spin stories just the way you want them told is, in a word, *perfect*.

A seven-time finalist for the prestigious Romance Writers of America RITA® Award, Maureen is the author of more than one hundred romance novels. Her books regularly appear on bestseller lists and have won several awards, including a Prism Award, a National Reader's Choice Award, a Colorado Award of Excellence and a Golden Quill.

One of her books, *The Soul Collector*, was made into a CBS-TV movie starring Melissa Gilbert, Bruce Greenwood and Ossie Davis. If you look closely, in the last five minutes of the movie you'll spot Maureen, who was an extra in the last scene.

Maureen believes that laughter goes hand in hand with love, so her stories are always filled with humor. The many letters she receives assures her that her readers love to laugh as much as she does.

Maureen Child is a native Californian, but has recently moved to the mountains of Utah. She loves a new adventure, though the thought of having to deal with snow for the first time is a little intimidating.

For my daughter, Sarah,
for so many reasons.
I love you.

One

"What do you call a female Peeping Tom?"

Griffin King didn't really expect an answer to the question since, for the moment, he was alone.

Still, it was an interesting puzzle.

Sprawled out comfortably in his cousin Rafe's hot tub, Griffin took a sip of his beer. Sliding his gaze to the short fence and the neighbor beyond, he watched as Nicole Baxter trudged in and out of her garage carrying what looked like *tons* of potting soil.

Seriously, he'd never seen a woman more focused on work. Most of the women he knew didn't do anything more strenuous than stretch out on a massage table. But Nicole…she was different.

He'd first met her more than a year ago, when his cousin Rafe married Nicole's next-door neighbor Katie Charles the Cookie Queen. Griffin smiled to himself. Katie was still running her cookie business and, bless her, had left a few dozen cookies for Griffin to eat while he was staying at their house.

But back to Nicole, he told himself with another sip of his beer. Despite the number of times he had been at Rafe's place, he had hardly spoken to Nicole. All he really knew about her was that she was divorced, a single mom and absolutely seemed to never stop working. Hell, she could give some of the Kings lessons in drive and determination. Made him tired just watching her.

Yet he couldn't seem to look away.

Maybe it was the whole forbidden fruit thing— the woman he couldn't have was the one who fascinated him? Possible, he told himself. Although it could just be that everything about her appealed to him.

Shaking his head, Griffin took off his sunglasses and set them on the edge of the redwood tub. The afternoon sun was bright, but he was shaded by a giant elm tree that grew between Nicole's house and the one he was currently living in.

Rafe and Katie were off on a three-week trip to Europe and Griffin had volunteered to house-sit. It hadn't been a completely altruistic offer. Since Griffin's beachside condo was for sale, the constant stream of lookie-loos prowling through his place on a daily basis was making him nuts. So staying here kept him sane and Rafe and Katie's place occupied.

A win-win anyway you looked at it.

Unless you counted Nicole.

His gaze followed her as she strode across the yard. Her shoulder-length blond hair was tucked behind her ears. She wore a pink tank top and cutoff jean shorts with a few dangling blue threads lying against her tanned, really exceptional thighs. Her skin was a sun-kissed pale gold and her curves were enough to make Griffin enjoy the view—a lot.

Knowing she was watching him back was a

nice plus that would ordinarily have had him inviting her over to join him in the hot tub. Ordinarily. But in Nicole's case, there were a couple of perfectly good reasons why he wasn't going to be getting any closer to her than he was right now.

"Mommy!"

"Speak of a reason," Griffin murmured. He took a long drink of the icy beer.

Nicole's nearly three-year-old son, Connor, was a cute kid, with big blue eyes and blond hair just like his mother. And Griffin didn't have anything against kids. Hell, he had more nephews, nieces and infant cousins than he knew what to do with. The King family was really taking the old *Go forth and multiply* thing to new levels.

What Griffin *did* have a problem with was getting involved with single moms. Frowning to himself, he tightened his grip on the cold can in his hand. He admired the hell out of a woman who could run her life, hold down a job *and* be both mother and father to a child. But he didn't do permanent, and when you inserted yourself into a child's world, there were bound to be complications.

He'd learned that years ago.

So Griffin's one main rule was *no women with kids*.

"Though for the first time," he said to himself, "breaking a rule looks really tempting."

"What is it, Connor?" Nicole's voice floated in the warm, late-June air. As busy as she always was, Griffin had never heard an edge of tired impatience in her voice.

"Wanna dig," the little boy shouted and waved a lime-green plastic trowel in the air like a Viking with a sword.

Griffin grinned, thinking about just how many holes he and his brothers had dug in their mother's flowerbeds. And how many hours of penance they'd all paid for every dead rose and daisy.

"Soon, sweetie," Nicole told the boy and tossed a quick glance over the fence at Griffin.

He lifted his beer in salute.

She frowned, shook her head and turned back to her son. "Let Mommy get the trays of plants from the garage, okay?"

"Need some help?" Griffin shouted.

She shifted her gaze back to him. Wryly, she

said, "I wouldn't want to tear you away from the hot tub."

Griffin smiled. She made it sound like he was hosting a drunken orgy. "Oh, I can always get back in."

"So it seems," she muttered, then said more loudly, "that's okay, Griffin. I can do it."

"All right then. If you change your mind, give a shout. I'll be right here."

"Where you are every day," she muttered.

"What was that?" he asked, though he'd heard her just fine.

"Nothing," she said and headed for her garage, her son racing after her like a much-shorter shadow.

Grinning, Griffin had another drink of his beer. He knew what Nicole thought of him. *Lazy* was no doubt first in her mind, which sort of bothered him, since this was the first vacation he'd taken in five years.

The security firm he and his twin, Garrett, owned and operated was the biggest of its kind in the world—which meant the King brothers were always on call. Well, they had been, until

Garrett had married Princess Alexis of Cadria several months back. Now Garrett ran their European operation and Griffin had control of the U.S. business.

But even workaholics needed a break eventually, and Griffin had decided to take his now—while a real-estate agent was parading people through his beachside condo. He had no idea yet where he'd move—he wanted to stay somewhere close to the beach. Maybe a place like Rafe and Katie's. All he knew for sure was that his condo had suddenly seemed a little too…sterile for him. Tastefully decorated by a woman Griffin had once dated, the place had never really felt like a home, and with Garrett making some major changes in his life, it had struck Griffin that maybe it was time he did some changing of his own.

He scowled to himself and took another drink of his beer.

Strange that he hadn't realized it before now, but Garrett getting married had precipitated all of the recent changes in Griffin's life. Not that he was in any hurry to race down an aisle or anything. All he wanted to do was shake up things in his life a little. Get a new house. Take a vacation.

That last part wasn't working out so well, though. He'd only been "relaxing" at Rafe and Katie's house for a few days and already he was getting itchy for something to do. He phoned the office so often—just to check on things—that his assistant had actually threatened to quit if he didn't stop calling.

It wasn't that he didn't trust his people. It was just that with nothing to do, nothing to accomplish, Griffin was quietly going a little whacked. He was coming to realize that he had *no idea* how to relax. He just wasn't made to sit still and do nothing. In fact, Garrett had bet him five hundred dollars that Griffin's vacation wouldn't last ten days, that he'd be racing back to work and burying himself in timetables and schedules.

Since Griffin wasn't about to willingly lose a bet, that wager pretty much insured that he was going to take his full three weeks off even if it killed him.

It just might.

Frowning, he took another sip of beer. What the hell did people *do* when they weren't working?

He knew what he'd *like* to do, he thought, letting his gaze slide over Nicole's trim, curvy body again. But it wasn't only Nicole's son that had Griffin dialing down his impulses. It was the fact that Rafe's wife, Katie, had made it plain a year ago—to *all* of the King cousins—that Nicole was off-limits. Hell, he could practically hear her even now.

"Nicole has been through a lot, with her rat bastard of an ex-husband," Katie had said, giving each of the King men at her engagement party a hard look. "So none of you are going to make a move on her, okay? I don't want my best friend getting hurt by a member of my new family."

And since there were millions of available women in the world, the King cousins had agreed to steer clear of Nicole Baxter. It hadn't been a hardship for Griffin, of course, because of the single-mother thing. At least, it hadn't until recently. The problem was, he thought, that he had too much free time. With nothing to do, naturally his brain was going to wander to a pretty woman.

And of course his body was only too willing to remind him that he'd been so busy since Garrett's marriage that dating and sex had taken a backseat.

It didn't help the situation any to know that while he was watching Nicole, *she* was watching *him*. And it wasn't irritation he saw on her features as much as attraction. He wasn't an idiot. He could tell when a woman was interested in him. Usually, he'd be the first one to make a move in this situation.

Pretty woman. Close proximity. All good.

And at least then he'd have something to *do*.

But he knew boredom wasn't Nicole's problem. The woman seemed to be constantly in motion. When she came back out of the garage, awkwardly balancing a huge tray of brightly colored flowers, Griffin scowled. No doubt she wouldn't thank him for his help, but he couldn't just stay where he was and watch while she staggered under the heavy weight. He set his beer down and bolted from the hot tub. He was across the patio and through the gate separating the two yards an instant later.

"Give me those," he said, snatching the surprisingly heavy flat from her.

Nicole swayed a bit when he took the carefully balanced weight from her so quickly. But she recovered fast. Lifting her gaze to his, she said, "I don't need your help. I can manage on my own."

"Yeah, I know," Griffin said amiably. "You are woman. You don't need a man. Let's just pretend we had this argument already and that you won. Now, where do you want me to put these?"

He glanced around the yard, spotted the bags of potting soil and headed for them. The grass was warm and soft under his bare feet and water ran in rivulets down his legs from the hem of his bathing suit. The sun felt good on his back, in spite of the fact that he also felt Nicole's gaze firing jagged pieces of ice at him.

Setting the tray down, he straightened up and turned to find her standing where he'd left her, across the yard, Connor's hand in hers. The tiny boy was grinning at him, but Nicole wasn't. Shaking his head, Griffin asked, "That wasn't so bad, was it?"

"What?"

"Accepting help," he said.

"I suppose not, and I should thank you even though I didn't ask for your help or need it," Nicole told him.

"Well, very gracious. You're welcome."

He laughed a little and headed back toward the fence, the hot tub and his beer. She'd made it clear enough that he wasn't welcome on her side of the fence. So if he needed something to do later, he'd call his assistant again and bug the hell out of her.

He was almost to the gate when her voice stopped him.

"Griffin, wait."

He looked over his shoulder at her.

"You're right," she said. "I did need the help and I do appreciate it."

Smiling, he said, "I think we're having a moment here."

She laughed and Griffin felt a solid punch of desire slam into him. The soft sound of her laughter spilled out around him. Her eyes lit with amusement and the wariness he was used to seeing glint out at him was gone.

"No moment," she said after a second or two. "But definitely a truce."

"Also good," he admitted and leaned one arm on the top of the gate. He watched Connor run to get his plastic shovel, then he shifted his gaze back to the boy's mother. "So, want to tell me why we need a truce in the first place?"

A soft breeze twisted a long strand of hair across her eyes and she reached up to tuck it behind her ears. "Okay, maybe *truce* was the wrong word." She looked over her shoulder to check on Connor, then turned her gaze back to Griffin. "It's just, I know Katie and I'm guessing she asked you to look out for me while they were gone and—"

"Nope." He cut her off with a shake of his head.

"Really?" She didn't sound convinced.

Griffin watched her, watched the breeze play with her hair and make the dangling blue threads from the hem of her shorts dance. Her nose was pink from the sun, her eyes were as deep a blue as the bowl of sky above them and there was a niggling, gnawing sensation inside him that was hunger. For her.

To remind himself, as well as to put her at ease, he said, "Okay, not completely true. Katie did ask me to keep an eye on the neighborhood—which would, of course, include you. But specifically?" He paused and shook his head. "Katie actually warned us all to keep our distance from you."

"Us all? Who all?"

"Us," he said. "The King cousins."

"She did not." Surprise flickered briefly in her eyes, followed quickly by a flash of outrage.

"Oh, yeah, she did. When she married Rafe, Katie made it clear that you were off-limits."

"Isn't that nice?" she muttered under her breath.

He lifted both hands. "Hey, wasn't me. I'm just saying…you've got nothing to worry about. I'm not about to cut off my own cookie supply by hitting on Katie's friend."

Although, Griffin had to admit, at least privately, that being this close to Nicole might have convinced him to give up his lifetime cookie connection just for a taste of her. If she hadn't been a mother.

Nicole wouldn't want to give up the cookies, either. After all, Katie made the best cookies in

California. Possibly in the world. But at the same time, it wasn't easy to know that a man would just as soon keep open his pipeline of chocolate chip goodies as take a bite out of you.

Still, knowing the truth explained a lot, she thought. Ever since her best friend Katie had married into the King family, there had been a steady stream of gorgeous, rich, single men in and out of the house next door. And every last one of those men had treated Nicole like a little sister. Heck, they'd done everything but pat her on the head.

She'd begun to believe she'd morphed into some kind of sexless, uninteresting blob. Not that she was looking for a man. Not a permanent one, at any rate. She'd already tried that and had found her ex-husband had the shelf life of an overripe tomato. No, she didn't want a man, but she didn't mind being flirted with occasionally, and the lack of interest from the King men had baffled her.

Now at least she knew what had been going on.

Oh, she could understand Katie's motivations. Her friend was being protective and a part of Nicole appreciated it. But seriously? She was a grown woman with a son, a home, a business all her own. She could take care of herself.

"She didn't have to do that," Nicole said at last.

He shrugged. "Looking out for a friend? Understandable. Especially since my cousin Cordell treated Katie herself so badly she almost didn't give Rafe a chance at all."

Nicole remembered that all too well. Katie had sworn off all King men because of her experience with one of them. Rafe hadn't told her his real last name until he and Katie were already involved.

"Your cousin Cordell is a dog."

"Agreed," he said amiably. "Always has been, too. Women seem to love him, though, which I can't figure out. Still, there's always the hope that he'll meet some woman who will give him the same treatment he's been handing out for years."

"There's a happy thought," Nicole said.

"Yeah." He paused, clearly enjoying the possibilities, which made Nicole smile.

"So anyway," he continued, "Katie was just looking out for you, I guess. And when she used the threat of a cookie cutoff, she got our attention. We do like our cookies."

As annoying as it might be to know that her best friend was running interference for her, Nicole couldn't really be angry at Katie for having good intentions.

"They are good cookies," she admitted.

"Exactly," Griffin agreed and gave her a smile that made something inside her sizzle and spark like a short fuse on a skyrocket. Honestly, every last one of the King men was a temptation to women everywhere.

But Griffin...he was danger, temptation and seduction on a whole new level. There was something about him—the smile, maybe, or the casual air he had—that made her feel things she hadn't experienced in, oh...forever. Okay, not that long, but long enough.

Nicole had spent the last few days surreptitiously watching him. After all, he was hard to miss, since he spent nearly every waking moment—practically naked—in that damn hot tub she could see from her backyard. Besides, she would have dared any living, breathing woman to *avoid* watching him—impossible really, since he looked amazing, with all that black hair and the blue eyes and a dimple—not to mention the sharply defined abs that practically *begged* a woman to stroke and caress his skin and...

Okay, she was clearly getting off track here. But who wouldn't be, she asked herself. With Griffin King standing not two feet from her, dripping wet, his board shorts dipping low enough on his hips to make her wonder what it might be like to give them a little tug and...

God.

"Are you going into a fugue state or something?" Griffin asked.

"Huh? What?" *Oh, perfect, Nicole. Get caught mentally slavering over him. Nice.* "No, I'm fine. Just busy."

"Yeah, I've noticed." He rubbed one palm across his chest and her gaze followed the motion.

Damn it. It was like being hypnotized by testosterone.

"Don't you ever just sit down in the shade?" he

asked, then stretched lazily. His chest muscles shifted; his board shorts dipped a little lower.

Nicole swallowed hard, closed her eyes briefly, then said, "No time." Just saying it reminded her how busy she really was.

Running her own business meant she could work most mornings and spend afternoons doing the million and one things that constantly needed doing around the house. But somehow weekends were still jam-packed. Amazing how chores stacked up. Plus, there was Connor. She glanced at her beautiful boy and smiled. It wasn't just the house she had to concentrate on. It was spending time with Connor. Making sure her son knew that he was the most important person in the world to her.

So yeah, her days were really crowded, unlike some Kings-who-reclined-in-hot-tubs.

"Connor's digging."

She didn't even look. "Of course he is. A little boy. A shovel. Dirt."

"You're a good mom."

Surprised, she looked up into Griffin's eyes. "Thanks. I try."

"It shows."

Gazes locked, a couple of humming seconds passed as they stared at each other. Nicole broke first.

"Well, I'd better get back to it."

"Planting," he said.

"Yes, but first, changing the lightbulb in the kitchen." She checked on Connor, then looked back at the man standing way too close to her. "Would you mind keeping an eye on him while I get the ladder from the garage?"

"Ladder?" He frowned.

"Kitchen light? Ceiling?"

He nodded. "You watch Connor. I'll get the ladder."

He was already headed for the garage when she called out, "You don't have to do that, I can—"

Lifting one hand to acknowledge her, he shouted back, "We've already had that conversation, remember? It's no problem."

"No problem," she muttered. Nicole shot a look at her son, happily digging holes.

It wasn't that she didn't appreciate the help. But Nicole had been on her own for a while now. She wasn't a delicate blossom. She knew how to fix plugged toilets and dripping sinks, and she took out her own garbage and killed her own spiders.

She didn't *need* a man's help.

But, a small voice in her mind whispered, was it really so bad to have it once in a while?

"Fine." She watched Griffin stride from the garage to the back door. The old wooden ladder was balanced on one shoulder and those darn board shorts of his looked to have dipped another inch or so. "He'll help, then he'll go home," she assured herself.

Then she could go back to watching him. From a safe distance.

"Where's the new lightbulb?"

"It's on the counter, Griffin—"

He shot her that fast, amazing grin again. "Be done in a minute."

No, he wouldn't. Her kitchen, like the rest of the small house her grandmother had left her, was old and out of date. The fluorescent lightbulb in the ancient fixture was three feet long and almost impossible to coax out of its fasteners, if you didn't know the little tricks to manage it. She'd have to help.

She glanced at her son. He was busy with his shovel. Just like the pirates in his favorite book, he was probably looking for buried treasure. She'd be able to see him from the kitchen window. "Connor, honey, you stay right there, okay?"

"'Kay!"

Hurrying into the kitchen after Griffin, Nicole saw that he already had the ladder positioned under the burned-out bulb. As he took one step up, the whole thing swayed and he looked down at her in amazement.

"You actually stand on this thing? Got a death wish?"

"It works fine," Nicole argued, somehow feeling as if she had to defend her late grandfather's ladder. She was pretty sure it was as old as the house, but it was perfectly serviceable. "You just weigh more than I do."

"If you say so," he muttered, and climbed up another couple of steps, still swaying like he was standing on the prow of a boat. "I'll have the old bulb out in a second."

"It's not easy," she said. "You have to wiggle to the left twice, then back to the right and once more to the left."

"It's a lightbulb, not a combination lock."

"That's what you think," Nicole told him, trying to keep from staring at his flat abdomen— which just happened to be at eye level. It had been way too long, Nicole thought, if just being this close to Griffin King was making her feel a little weak in the knees.

Damn it, she knew better. Griffin, like every other King, was a player. A master of flirtation and seduction. And didn't *that* sound interesting, her mind whispered.

Her mind drifted as she considered tugging at his board shorts just a little. Dragging them down until—

"I've got it," he grumbled, shaking her out of her thoughts, thank heaven.

"Be careful." She frowned up at him, but he was too busy with the light to notice. "Remember to wiggle to the left first."

"It's just. A. Little. Stubborn." He yanked the

bad bulb out and held it one hand triumphantly. "Hah!"

A small, blond torpedo raced through the open back door. Connor was running so fast he never saw the ladder until he crashed into it.

Nicole let go of the ladder to grab her son.

The ladder swayed sharply to the right.

Griffin's balance dissolved and he reached up with his free hand to grab the light fixture to steady himself.

He pulled it right out of the ceiling.

His eyes went wide.

Nicole gasped.

Chunks of old plaster fell down on them like hail.

Connor wailed.

The ladder tipped farther.

Griffin toppled to one side, then jumped, still clutching the remnants of the light fixture he'd yanked free.

Pop. Pop. Pop.

Three little sounds.

Nicole looked up to see a wisp of smoke and the first flames erupt. "Oh, God!"

"Everybody out!" Griffin dropped the lightbulb and grabbed hold of Nicole and Connor, steering them out the back door to safety.

Two

The firemen were very nice.

They let Connor wear one of their helmets and sit in the big truck, while an older fireman kept watch.

Nicole was grateful. She needed a minute. Or two. Or maybe thirty. She sighed as she let her gaze slide from her son to the mess that was her house. Fire hoses were stretched across the lawn, now muddy from too much water and too many feet. Neighbors were gathered around watching the excitement—even Mr. Hannity, who had to be a hundred and ten, had pried himself off his front porch to get a better view. And Griffin was talking to one of the firemen like they were old friends.

Standing alone at the end of her driveway, Nicole listened halfheartedly to the conversations and noise around her. There was a buzzing in her ears that she thought might be the personification of the panic beginning to chew at her insides.

Her knees were still a little shaky and her stomach did an occasional slow roll. Probably leftover adrenaline still pumping through her system. Griffin had moved so fast, snatching Connor from her, then grabbing hold of her arm to pull her out of the kitchen. Thank God she kept her cell phone in her pocket. She'd used it to call the fire department the moment they were clear of the house.

Her *house*.

She hadn't been back inside yet. Didn't even know if she *wanted* to go look at the disaster that was now her kitchen. Nicole could only imagine what she'd find, and her imagination was pretty darn good. And while those dismal thoughts were spinning through her mind, more piled on for the trip.

Insurance.

Of course the house was insured, but there was a huge deductible—to make the payments easier to live with. And now, thinking of trying to meet that deductible was giving Nicole cold chills in spite of the sun beating down on her shoulders.

How was she going to pay for this?

How could she not?

"Jim says it's not too bad, considering."

"Huh? What?" Nicole looked up at Griffin, surprised to find him standing right in front of her. Her mind really was tangled up in knots of misery if she hadn't noticed his approach.

He tipped his head to one side and studied her. "Another fugue state? Or shock? Maybe you should sit down."

"I don't want to sit down," she said. In fact, what she *wanted* to do was throw herself onto the grass and kick and scream for a while. But since that wasn't going to happen, she asked, "I want to find out what shape my house is in and see if it's safe."

"Jim says it is."

"The fireman you were talking to?"

"Yeah." Griffin shrugged. "Don't get your feminist temper rolling. I didn't head him off to get information. I went to school with him, can you believe that coincidence? Jim Murphy. He's a fire captain now. Married, got a million kids…"

"All very nice for Jim," Nicole said tightly. "What did he say about my kitchen?"

"Oh." The smile dropped from his face. "He'll be over to talk to you in a minute. He's just checking the place out again before they wrap things up and leave."

"So the fire's out."

"Absolutely," he assured her, and reached out to lay one hand on her shoulder briefly. "Electrical, but you knew that."

Yes. She'd probably be hearing that series of pops in her dreams for weeks.

"Apparently your wiring's shot," Griffin told her.

"It was working fine until today," she argued, even though she knew he was right. The wiring was old; the pipes were antiques. But there just never seemed to be enough money to fix everything. She'd made plans, of course. Big plans, for a remodel of the kitchen, for adding a huge bath onto the master bedroom. Maybe a deck off the kitchen…but they were just plans. Pie in the sky, as her grandmother used to say.

"Yeah, and I feel really bad about that," Griffin said, bringing her back to the conversation. "If I hadn't tugged on the light fixture…"

A part of her wanted to agree. That angry, desperate voice inside her wanted to shout, *I told you I didn't need any help!* But sadly, fury wasn't going to change anything. She shook her head and waved one hand, dismissing his guilt. "Things happen. Nothing to do about it now, anyway."

In fact, she was lucky Griffin hadn't fallen off the ladder and cracked his skull, too. Then she'd be dealing not only with fire damage but doctor bills, as well.

"Besides," she said, turning her gaze to look at Connor, grinning at her from under the huge helmet he was still wearing, "we're all safe. That's what counts."

"Good attitude," Griffin said, and turned when Jim Murphy walked up to join them.

"Ms. Baxter," he said and shook her hand. "The

house is safe for you to enter again, but I wouldn't advise staying there until you've had all of the wiring checked by an electrician."

"Right," she mumbled. "But the fire's out? It's not going to spring back into life?"

He smiled and shook his head. "No, it won't. The power's been shut off to the kitchen circuits. But because of the age of the house, that circuit also runs through half of the living room, so there's no power in there, either. Just to be safe, I'd have an electrician and a contractor check everything out before you turn the power back on."

"Of course." Professionals. Electricians. Contractors. Then there would be plasterers, painters...visions of dollar bills flying out an open window popped into Nicole's mind and she again fought the urge to kick and scream. Pushing the worry to the back of her mind, she forced a smile and said, "Thank you. I appreciate you getting here so quickly."

"Glad we could help," the man said and looked over his shoulder at the house. "It's built well. These old houses have good bones. I know it seems like a lot now, but," he added, turning back to smile at her, "it could have been a lot worse. As it is, once the main problem is fixed, you'll be good. There's no structural damage."

Small favors, Nicole thought.

"Thanks, Jim," Griffin said, shaking the other man's hand. "Good to see you. Say hi to Kathy for me, okay?"

"I'll do it." He walked toward the fire truck, and Griffin joined him. "Maybe we could do dinner some night, huh?"

Firemen were still moving around her lawn, rolling up hoses, talking, laughing together. The crowd of neighbors was breaking up, with only the nosiest lingering. Jim and Griffin were still catching up and Connor was now "steering" the big fire truck with a wild grin on his face.

Nicole had zoned out. Let the two old buddies make plans for beers and burgers. Let her son revel in little-boy daydreams. Right now, she was more concerned with what she was going to do next. The sad truth was, she had no clue.

"You okay?"

She glanced up, surprised to find that Griffin had joined her again. "Not so much."

"Yeah, I can understand that," he said, "but you've got insurance, right?"

"Of course I have insurance," she snapped, then bit her lip. It wasn't his fault she was in a mess. Well, she supposed technically it *was* his fault since he'd ripped the light fixture out of the ceiling while he was changing a bulb she hadn't asked him to change. But it wasn't as if he'd set out to burn down her kitchen.

"Then don't wind yourself up so tight," he advised. "You're safe. Connor's safe. The house can be fixed."

"I know," she said firmly, trying to convince herself more than him. It was true, after all. She'd find a way to get it done. She could maybe take a loan out on the house, though she really hated to do that. It was paid for and not having a mortgage payment every month was a blessing she never took for granted. Still, it wasn't as if she had a lot of options. She also didn't want to discuss any of this with Griffin.

"You're right. We're all safe. The rest will get handled. Now—" she looked over at the fire truck and her happy son "—I think I'll go collect Connor before he stows away on the truck and I never see him again."

"Okay, then, you want to go in and take a look?"

"Not really," she admitted.

"It'll be okay," Griffin said.

She looked up at him. "Have you ever noticed that people say that whenever things are absolutely *not* okay?"

"Good point. But not looking won't change anything."

"Also a good point." She sighed heavily and glanced at her house briefly before walking to the truck. There she retrieved her now-sulky son from the fireman who was his new best friend. When she walked back to Griffin, Connor on her hip, she said, "You don't have to go in with me."

He only looked at her for a long second, and in his eyes, she read plainly that he wasn't going anywhere. She didn't know whether to be relieved or pissed.

"Yeah, I do." He waved to the firemen, then followed her around the side of the house to the back.

Funny, just a couple of hours ago, she'd been

minding her own business, stealing peeks at a barely dressed Griffin while he lounged in a hot tub. Now they were banded together to inspect what she suspected was complete devastation.

Her stomach jumped with nerves and worry, but there was more than that, too. Thanks to Griffin's presence, she was even more on edge than she might have been. Nicole actually *felt* him behind her. It was almost like an electrical charge on the air.

Oh, God. Electrical charge.

Electrical wiring.

Fire.

Yeah, this was no time to be indulging in a hormonal surge.

She came around the corner of the house, saw the back door standing open and, for a second, could only think about the flies and bugs that were no doubt racing into the house. Then she realized insects were the least of her problems. She steeled herself for whatever she was going to find, then climbed the three short steps and went inside.

There was no way Nicole could have steeled herself enough.

The kitchen looked as if it had come through a hurricane. Water everywhere. Smoke stains on the ceilings and walls, like black shadows crawling across the paint. The ceiling itself was pretty much torn out. The plaster that had first rained down on them when Griffin pulled the fixture free was nothing compared to what the firemen had done to contain the fire.

Gaping holes stared back at her when she looked up, as if the house itself was glaring at her accusingly. Plaster dust and water, congealed into a heavy paste, littered the worn counters, and the floor was covered in the stuff.

"Oh. My. God."

She wanted to cry. And scream. And grab a shovel and a broom and start returning her world to normal. But as her gaze studied what was left of her ceiling, she knew it was going to take a lot more than elbow grease to get this job done.

"House is dirty!" Connor shouted, clapping both hands.

Instinctively, she tightened her grip on her son.

"It's a wreck," Griffin pointed out unnecessarily.

Nicole stood in one spot and did a slow turn, letting her horrified gaze take in the destruction. For the first time, she understood completely what the phrase *her heart sank* was referring to.

"I don't even know where to start to clean this up," she murmured, shifting a look through the open doorway into the living room. That room hadn't entirely escaped, either. Furniture had been pushed aside and puddles of water had gathered on the hardwood floor.

For one second, she remembered the last time her house had been flooded, when her pipes sprang a leak and Katie had rushed over to help, dragging Rafe King along with her. It was the first time she'd met Rafe. And now, here she was, her house was flooded and yet another King was on hand for the occasion.

"You don't have to clean it up," Griffin said from behind her.

"You see anyone else signing up for the job?" It would take her *hours,* she thought miserably.

"We'll get a cleaning crew in here," he suggested.

"I can't afford that," she argued.

"Well, you can't do it alone, and I'm not doing it," he said.

"Who asked for your help?" Nicole's temper, already frayed by the fire, began bubbling.

"Not you," Griffin said and folded his arms over his chest. Shaking his head, he blurted, "You wouldn't ask for help if you were neck-deep in quicksand and sinking fast, would you?"

"If you think that's insulting, you're wrong," she told him. "I can take care of myself. Been doing it for years."

"And because you *can* do it, you *should?*"

Connor squirmed again and rather than keep trying to hold on to him, she stalked past Griffin and walked out into the backyard. At least here she wasn't surrounded by what was left of her house. The cloying smell of wet smoke wasn't choking her. And she wasn't as tempted to sit down on the ground and cry just for the hell of it.

Setting Connor down, she watched him race off to the flowerbed and his beloved shovel. Sunlight played on his blond hair and his sturdy little legs pumped with his eagerness to get back to playing.

When Griffin walked up behind her, Nicole didn't even look at him. "I know you're trying to help, but it'd really be best if you just went home."

"Right." He moved to stand in front of her, forcing her to look up at him. Those blue eyes of his were fixed on her, daring her to look away. So of course she didn't. "You really think I'm just going to walk back to the house and hop back into the hot tub? Adventure over? End of story?"

"Why not?"

He laughed shortly. "I think I was just insulted, but we'll let that one go for now. What I can't figure out is if you're really this stubborn or if it's an act for my benefit."

Stunned, she stared at him. "Why would I do anything for your benefit, Griffin?"

"Just what I was asking myself," he muttered. "But if you're serious about this, it's just as crazy. I'm not going to leave you here alone with a two-year-old in the middle of this *wreck*."

She wasn't sure why he was upset. It wasn't

his house that had caught fire. "You don't get to decide that."

"Well, then, you should decide it. How are you going to manage with no power? No kitchen?"

Nicole didn't have an answer for that. Yet. She'd figure something out, though. She always had. Her gaze shifted to Connor, sitting in the shade, singing to himself as he piled dirt from the flowerbed onto the grass. Everything in her softened and toughened up at the same time. She would do whatever she had to. For her son. "This is my house, Griffin. Where else am I supposed to go?"

"Next door with me."

"What?" Her gaze shot to his.

He pushed one hand through his hair and this time Nicole was so stupefied by everything else around her that she barely noticed the flex of his muscles or the dip of his board shorts at the movement.

"The fire was my fault."

"True," she said, then shook her head when he winced. "I mean, no. It's not. Not completely."

One black eyebrow lifted and she idly wondered how people managed that. Then she sighed. "You were trying to help."

"And burned down your kitchen."

She gave him a wry smile. "I didn't say you *had* helped. I said you were trying."

He smiled, too. "Look, Rafe and Katie's place is huge."

"I know," Nicole said. "Ever since they got married, Katie complains that she's never sure what her house is going to look like from one day to the next. Rafe is always adding something or tearing something else out and building bigger..."

She'd never envied Katie the financial security she'd gained by marrying into the King family. But sometimes, late at night when she was alone, Nicole silently admitted to being jealous of the love Katie had found. The security of knowing she didn't have to handle everything on her own. She and Rafe were so good together that Nicole couldn't help wishing that somehow, someday, she might find that same kind of love for herself.

Of course, her romantic history read like a Greek tragedy, so she'd accepted the fact that the chances of that happening were slim to none.

But, she had always consoled herself, she had her son. Her business. Her home.

Well, until today she'd had a home. She looked over her shoulder at the house that wouldn't be livable for weeks.

"Nicole, you know it's the best answer. Hell, the house is so big, we won't be in each other's way." Griffin moved in closer. "You can't stay here. It's not safe. For you or for Connor."

"Probably not…"

Clearly exasperated, he asked, "You really want to live in a hotel while this place is fixed?"

No, she really didn't. Not only was the thought of trying to keep her nearly three-year-old son contained in a tiny hotel room exhausting, but there was the cost to consider. She couldn't afford to fix the kitchen *and* live in a hotel.

"Besides," Griffin added, "this way, you'll be close by while they're working on your place and you can stay on top of things."

True. All true. But she hated owing someone. She took care of herself and her son and she'd done a damn good job of it, if she had to be the one to say it. Depending on someone, accepting favors from anyone, was just something Nicole didn't do. Not anymore. Not since her ex-husband had taught her the hard way that the only person you could count on was yourself.

She looked up at Griffin and ground her teeth together. He looked so sure of himself, fresh irritation spiked inside her. Mainly because, though she didn't want to admit it, Nicole knew she didn't have a choice, and she *really* hated that.

But, she told herself, the truth was, if this had happened when Katie and Rafe were at home, Katie would have insisted that Nicole and Connor move in. So having Griffin extend the invitation wasn't really much different, was it?

Her mind laughed at the pitiful rationalization. Hmm. Happily married couple offering her a place to stay, or a matching offer from a gorgeous, single guy who made every one of her hormones stand up to do a fast boogie. Sure. Exactly the same situation.

Frowning, she pushed that thought aside.

Boogying had not been a part of the offer, sadly.

Besides, she reminded herself, Griffin *had* started the fire in her kitchen.

"You know it's the only solution," he said.

"Yeah, it is." Nodding, she glanced back at the kitchen and tried not to picture what it looked like in there. Instead, she imagined it after the work was done. Maybe, if it wasn't too expensive, she could upgrade it a little. Maybe this would turn out to be a good thing.

Then her gaze shifted to Griffin, who was watching her out of brilliant blue eyes. His tanned, muscled chest caught her attention for one wild second. If he had been temptation living next door…what was it going to be like living *with* him?

It was a nightmare.

The next morning, Griffin rubbed eyes gritty from lack of sleep and told himself he might as well get used to it. Sure, Rafe and Katie's house was big. But he'd been exaggerating a little when he'd assured Nicole that there was plenty of room for all of them.

He'd forgotten that all of the bedrooms led off the same hallway. His room was directly across the hall from Nicole's, and he could have sworn he heard every move she made during the night.

She'd paced, then sat on the bed with a telltale squeak. Then she'd been up and pacing again. Several times she opened her bedroom door and took the four steps to the room where Connor was sleeping. She'd open that door, walk across the wood floor, pause. Then back across the room, close the door and pace in her own room again.

Okay, it wasn't the noise that was bothering him. Hell, he'd been known to sleep through a fireworks display, complete with M-80 rockets. No, it had been picturing Nicole, blond hair tousled, bare feet whispering across the floor, that was doing it to him. He wondered what she slept in. Nightgown? T-shirt? *Nothing?* He'd seen enough of her body in the tank tops and shorts she wore to know that he'd like to see more.

Knowing he couldn't was annoying the hell out of him.

But he could do this. Play the white knight. Offer her sanctuary, a place to stay, and he could do it all without groping or seducing her. Didn't sound like much fun, but he could do it.

She was a mother, for God's sake. And then
there was Katie's threat to consider. Besides, he
was thirty-three now. That was the magic number. The age he'd decided would be the end of his
days as a player. The age when he would damn
well mature whether he wanted to or not.

"And I really don't want to."

"Are you talking to yourself?"

He glanced up as Nicole came into the kitchen,
Connor on her hip. She was wearing white shorts
and a bright pink tank top with matching pink
polish on her toes. Her hair was tucked behind
her ears and twin silver hoops winked at him in
the early sunlight.

"What? No." He shook his head and focused
on the cup of coffee he held between his palms.
"I'm just thinking."

"Wow, you're a noisy thinker."

Connor shouted, "Down!"

Griffin winced. It was too early for conversation and way too early for chipper.

"Want some milk, baby?" Nicole asked.

Griffin almost said *no thanks.*

Connor shouted, "*Milk!* And cookies!"

Nicole laughed. "No cookies for breakfast."

Griffin looked at the boy. Such a cute kid. Would it be wrong to put tape across his mouth?

Nicole brought Connor some milk, then took eggs from the fridge and a skillet from the cupboard. She was as comfortable in Katie's kitchen as she was in her own. "Can I make you something?"

"No, I never eat breakfast," he mumbled, concentrating on the coffee. Caffeine. The secret to survival.

"It's Connor's favorite meal," she said, and started scrambling eggs, setting the skillet on the stove and in general making a clatter of noise that had Griffin clenching his teeth.

"I've decided that I'm going to look at this whole situation as a gift," Nicole said from her place at the stove.

"Is that right?" Griffin reached out and took away the spoon Connor was beating against the tabletop. The little boy's features screwed up, his bottom lip poked out and a sheen of tears filled small blue eyes. Griffin sighed and handed the spoon back.

Just keep drinking coffee, he told himself and stood up to get a refill.

"Well, like you said," Nicole continued, "I have to have it fixed anyway, so I've decided to try and look at it like redecorating rather than rebuilding."

"Probably a good idea," he allowed as he took his seat again. Connor grinned at him and pounded that spoon with all the fervor of a rock-band drummer.

Griffin was *not* a morning person. He preferred conversations over a late supper with plenty of wine. He never spent the night with any of the women he...dated, so the morning-after chat had never been on his agenda. Now, not only did he have a woman to talk to, but a two-year-old to endure.

Usually he greeted morning with all the enthusiasm of a condemned prisoner facing execution. Today, even more so.

Nicole set scrambled eggs in front of Connor and the little boy used his fingers to eat while he continued to pound the spoon. Griffin sighed, then asked himself just when exactly he'd turned into an old crank.

"Connor has preschool," Nicole was saying, "so as soon as I drop him off, I'll be back here to make some phone calls to the insurance company and a contractor..."

Griffin took a sip of coffee. "You take care of calling the insurance company and I'll call King Construction," he offered. "They'll take care of it and give you a better deal than you'd get anywhere else."

He watched her and saw refusal glint in her eye a moment before she nodded and said, "Thanks. I appreciate that."

She might appreciate it, he told himself, but she also didn't like having to accept favors. He could understand that even as he would have swept right past her refusal if she had argued with him.

"No problem. What's the point of having family if you can't call on them when you need 'em? With Rafe out of town, I'll talk to Lucas. He can probably come over today for a look around."

"Okay." She handed Connor a cup of milk at

the same time Griffin slipped the spoon from the boy's hand.

"Not used to dealing with kids, are you?" she asked with a half smile.

"Not at the crack of dawn," he admitted, feeling a little guilty now at snatching away Connor's spoon again. Resigned, he gave it back.

"It's eight o'clock."

"My point exactly." When his world hadn't been turned upside down, Griffin would just now be sitting down for his first cup of coffee. He'd be on the balcony of his condo, staring out at the water, letting the silence sink into him. Then he'd shower, get dressed and arrive at King Security a little after nine.

Ironic, he thought, that his working schedule suddenly looked so much more relaxing than his vacation.

Shaking her head, Nicole focused on her son. Taking another sip of his coffee, Griffin watched her with the boy, saw her eyes sparkle with interest and humor as Connor prattled, half coherent, half in some weird baby speak that Nicole seemed to understand. Morning sunlight lay across the table and shone in her hair and something hot and hard settled in the pit of his stomach—then dropped lower. Any woman who could affect him like this first thing in the morning was dangerous.

Oh, yeah. Them living here together was going to work out great, he told himself with a heavy sigh.

He needed to make that call to King Construction fast. The quicker he got Nicole out of arm's reach, the better it would be.

For all of them.

Three

"Man, you did a number on this place." Lucas King moved through Nicole's kitchen later that afternoon, noting every bit of damage with a practiced eye, missing nothing. In minutes he had examined the room, checking every outlet, every piece of missing plaster. The power was still off, of course, but Lucas had checked that as well, not trusting anyone else's word for it.

"I didn't exactly put a torch to it," Griffin argued, leaning back against the ruined kitchen counter.

"Might as well have." Lucas's voice was muffled. Standing on a metal ladder, he had his head poked through the hole in the ceiling while he shifted the beam of his flashlight across the area.

Griffin thought about giving the ladder a shove, just on principle. But, since his cousin was actually using a *stable* ladder rather than the one Griffin had toppled off, it probably wouldn't do any good.

"You did all this by falling off a ladder?"

"Yeah," Griffin said tightly. He heard the amusement in his cousin's voice and knew damn well that Lucas would be telling this story to the rest of the family. "I grabbed the light fixture, hoping to steady myself, and instead…"

Lucas snorted. "Ripped it right out of the wall, didn't you?"

"Seriously?" Scowling at his cousin's back, Griffin added, "I didn't bring you here to rag on me. Just to look at the kitchen."

"Yeah, I know," Lucas said, voice still muffled as he continued his examination. "The ragging on you is the fun part of all this."

"Happy to help," Griffin said in a tone that made it plain he *wasn't* happy. "How bad is it?"

"Like a bad horror movie up here. The wiring

is antique," Lucas muttered. "Even from a distance I can see spots that are frayed. It's a wonder the place didn't catch fire years ago."

That thought gave Griffin cold chills. He thought of Nicole and her son living here alone. What if there'd been an electrical fire in the middle of the night? Even with the smoke alarms, there was no guarantee Nicole and Connor would have gotten out. He scraped one hand across his face as a sense of uneasiness rolled through the pit of his stomach.

"Guess we can't lay this one all on you," Lucas commented as he came down the ladder, metal groaning and creaking with his every step, to stand in the center of the devastated kitchen.

He squinted into the sunlight streaming through the window over the sink. "The wiring in the whole damn house is about a breath away from whoosh."

Griffin shook his head. "Whoosh?"

"That's a technical term." Lucas grinned. "The sound a fire makes when it whooshes into life."

"Great. Disaster humor." Griffin didn't think it was funny. He'd actually *heard* that sound, right after the series of pops when the wiring burst into flame. He remembered the smell of the smoke, too, and tried to push those memories out of his mind. The kitchen was wrecked, but they'd all gotten out in one piece. That was the important part. And from what Lucas was saying, they were lucky the whole house hadn't been turned into a pile of rubble.

Griffin pushed away from the counter and tucked his hands into his pockets. He took a quick look around the room and saw things he hadn't noticed when he'd been here before—pictures of Connor on the fridge. A teakettle in the shape of a rooster on the soot-covered stove. Small green glass vases, knocked off the windowsill, now shattered on the scarred countertop, the flowers they'd held lying wilted and dead beside them.

It wasn't just a room, he thought, it was Nicole's *home,* and more of a home than he had. Visions of his condo leaped into his mind. Hell, all he ever used the place for was to store his clothes, to sleep and occasionally to nuke a takeout dinner. He frowned to himself as a nibble of guilt chewed at him. She'd lost so much, and he had more than he needed or used.

Didn't seem to matter that Lucas had told him the wiring was ready to blow at any time. The plain truth was, Griffin had pulled those wires loose. Griffin had caused the damn fire that had put Nicole and her son out of their house. And *Griffin* was the one who had to make it right.

Whether Nicole liked it or not.

"So what do you want to do?" Lucas asked, making notes on a computer tablet.

"I want her place fixed."

"We can do that," his cousin assured him. "I'm assuming she's got insurance?"

"She says so," Griffin told him. "But I'm guessing she's got a big deductible, too."

"Probably." Lucas nodded thoughtfully. "Single moms don't usually have a hell of a lot of extra cash lying around."

"That's what I think, too." Griffin glanced over at the house next door, where Nicole was working in the dining room with her laptop—thankfully undamaged by either the fire or water. She knew Lucas was here, but she hadn't been in a hurry to walk back through the destruction, so she had stayed where she was, waiting to talk to Lucas when the inspection was over.

Turning back to his cousin, he said, "I'll take care of the deductible and any extra it runs."

Lucas's eyebrows lifted. "Is that right?"

Griffin saw the interested look in his cousin's eyes and sneered. "Don't get any ideas. There's nothing going on between me and Nicole. But I caused this. The least I can do is fix it."

"She won't like it."

"She doesn't have to know."

Lucas laughed shortly. "Dude, you are out of your mind if you really think Nicole won't find out what you're up to."

"Please." Griffin tugged his hands from his pockets and folded his arms over his chest. "I'm in the security business, remember? We know how to keep secrets."

"Not from women you don't." Lucas shook his head. "It's spooky, I swear. Every time I think I put one over on Rose, she nails me with it. It's like female radar or something. Built into the whole double X chromosome or whatever."

Griffin just stared at him. "You're delusional."

"No, I'm married."

"Same thing."

"You're a sad, sad man," Lucas said, shaking his head and grinning.

"Yeah," Griffin shot back, his smile wide and self-satisfied. "Poor me. Different woman every week. Nobody making demands on my time. Sex whenever I want it."

"Uh, hello?" Lucas scowled at him. "I get sex whenever I want it, too, you know. *And* I don't have to leave home to get it."

"Yeah?" Griffin laughed. "How's the sex life these days?"

Lucas's wife was pregnant with their second child. Just like most of the King family, Lucas had turned from a player into a husband and father. The Kings were falling, one by one, like a row of dominoes bowing to gravity. Pitiful. Just pitiful.

"You should have it so good." Lucas gave him a wicked grin.

Possibly true. For all his big talk, Griffin knew that his cousin had a point. Hell, over the last few months, Griffin had been less and less interested in living the lifestyle that had been his for years. Dozens of different women had come and gone from his life, barely making an impression. *Different.* He laughed silently at that, because though the faces and names had changed, they'd all been the same.

Beautiful and boring.

Try having a conversation with any of them. Hell, after the first five minutes, he'd been zoned out and barely listening to talk that centered on the hottest club, the newest designer or the best place to get a spray-on tan.

But then, he hadn't dated them for their ability to discuss art and literature, had he? Griffin could admit that all he'd wanted from them—*any* of them—was a quick romp in the sheets. So he really had no room for complaints, did he?

Damn. This whole maturing thing was a pain in the ass.

"So when do you want us to get started?" Lucas asked with another glance around the kitchen.

"This afternoon work for you?"

Lucas laughed. "Got it. You want it done fast."

Nodding, he made a few notes on his computer tablet. "We're spread a little thin right now—we've got at least a half dozen jobs up and running, not to mention that Rosie's got me building shelves in Danny's room when I'm not working. But two of our jobs are winding down."

"Man. Rafe left town for a vacation when you've got that much work piled up?" Out of character for a King, Griffin thought.

"Yeah, well." Lucas shrugged. "Things change when you've got a wife and a *life*. Besides, Rafe wanted to take Katie on that tour of Europe while she was still feeling well enough to travel."

"Katie?" Fear reached up and closed a hand around the base of Griffin's throat. Staring at his cousin, he demanded, "Is there something wrong with Katie? Why doesn't the family know about it?"

"Damn it." Lucas lifted one hand. "Power down. Nothing's wrong with Katie. She's pregnant, is all. And nobody's supposed to know yet, so keep your big mouth shut. Katie and Rafe are gonna have a family deal when they get back and let everybody know."

Relief spilled through Griffin. "I already told you, I know how to keep a secret."

"Right." Lucas nodded. "Anyway, Rafe wanted them to have some time together before their lives really get busy. Nothing sucks up your time like kids."

Another King becoming a father. Finding a life. Finding…something more. Something that Griffin wasn't sure he'd ever find for himself and, if he did, he didn't know that he'd want it. Which said what, exactly, about him? Griffin frowned to himself.

"Another King bites the dust," he muttered to cover up the unexpected emotions crowding him.

"Call it what you want," Lucas said, a little on the defensive side. "But we don't see it that way."

"You used to," Griffin reminded him. "In fact," he continued, "I remember a poker game a few years ago when we were talking about Adam and Travis getting married and you said—"

Lucas huffed out a breath. "I remember."

"—you said," Griffin went on, "that getting married was like being buried, only you didn't have the sense to lie down and be dead."

Shaking his head, Lucas muttered, "Yeah, well, things change."

"Damn straight they do," Griffin told him, and felt his own wayward emotions coming back into line. Maturing was one thing, he told himself sternly. Going crazy over one woman and signing up for a lifetime of marriage was something else again. He wasn't about to set himself up to be one of the many Kings ready for a fall. Let his cousins go from happy bachelors to husbands and fathers. Let his own *twin,* for God's sake, make that move, but not him. "Things change, cousin, but only if you *let* them."

Lucas snorted. "Whatever you say, cuz."

Griffin knew sarcasm when he heard it. "Just figure out who you can get in here to fix up this place. And do it fast."

"You got it," Lucas said. "We'll take care of permits from the city. I'll have some plans drawn up and email them to Nicole for approval." He turned off the tablet and tucked it beneath his arm. "Tell her I'll let her know when she needs to decide on flooring, paint and appliances."

"Fine." And whatever she picked, Griffin promised silently, he'd be upgrading. He paid his debts, and he'd be damned if he was going to let Nicole have a half-assed remodel because of her pride.

Chuckling softly, Lucas headed for the back door. "You know…sometimes things change whether you want them to or not. And not even a King can stop it."

Griffin didn't bother saying aloud what he was thinking. *You can stop anything—if you never let it get started.*

Trouble was, Griffin told himself as he walked out of the destruction into the summer sunlight, as far as Nicole was concerned, he had a feeling it was already too late.

Something had already started between them.

Putting the brakes on might not be as easy as he'd like.

Nothing said summer more than the scent of hamburgers on a grill.

Nicole stepped out of Katie's kitchen, carrying a bowl of potato salad and a plate filled with sliced tomatoes, onions and cheese for the burgers Griffin was flipping on the grill.

Her gaze slid across the grass until she spotted her son, playing in the sandbox table Griffin had retrieved from her yard. Connor was completely entranced with pushing his toy dinosaurs through sand mountains, so she set the potato salad down under the umbrella shading the redwood table, then she walked to Griffin.

She studied him as she got closer and, as usual, her gaze did the up-and-down thing until she'd examined every really gorgeous inch of him. He was wearing those board shorts again and his bare back was broad and tanned to a dark gold. His hips were narrow, his muscular legs long, and his black hair curled at the nape of his neck.

A flutter of something interesting wafted through her and Nicole had to take a deep breath to steady herself. Seriously, didn't the man own a shirt?

"Dinner's almost ready," he said as she approached.

"Good. I'm starving." In more ways than one, she realized.

"Barbecuing is the one kind of cooking I can

do without having to call the fire department."
As soon as he said it, he winced. "Sorry."

"It's okay." She waved off the apology even as
she shrugged off the memories the mention of
the fire department had caused. After all, it had
only been a single day since her house had become uninhabitable. Not surprising that she was
still a little touchy on the subject of fire. Heck,
she hadn't even watched Griffin as he turned on
the propane flames on the barbecue.

"Lucas emailed me a brief proposal," she said,
setting the plate of cheese and vegetables down
on the workbench alongside the truly impressive
grill Rafe had built the summer he and Katie first
got together.

She thought about Lucas's proposal and had to
muffle a whine. Even cutting the cost down to
the bone—which she knew Lucas had done because of Nicole's friendship with Katie King—
the total had staggered her. She was going to
have to either take out a small home-equity loan
to cover her deductible, or maybe she could work
out a payment schedule with King Construction.
Something to think about, anyway.

"Good." Griffin glanced at her, then turned his attention back to the burgers on the grill. He reached for the cheese and slapped a slice on each burger. "Lucas said he could have a crew out here starting the teardown as early as tomorrow."

"Teardown." She sighed a little at the image those words created. Then she looked up to find Griffin watching her.

"Then they'll start the redo," he said softly. "Does that make it easier?"

Not really. "I suppose."

He dropped one hand onto her shoulder and the heat of his touch sent a wave of warmth radiating through her body.

"Lucas promised to get the job done as fast as he could."

"I know." She looked over the fence at her house and couldn't help thinking that it looked...lonely. For the first time in her memory, the house was empty, and Nicole's world was still shaken. "I appreciate you getting him to do it this quickly."

"Not a problem. I did have a hand in you needing the kitchen redone."

"Yeah," she agreed, "you did."

He winced.

"But from what your friend Jim the fireman said, the wiring was poised to go at any moment."

"Lucas will take care of that, too. He's got a master electrician who will fix all the wiring and just tack it onto the cost of the kitchen redo."

Fabulous. An inner shriek resounded loudly, but at the same time, Nicole had to admit that the house definitely needed rewiring. She'd never be able to sleep soundly in her bed again if she was lying there every night, terrified that a fire would erupt and endanger her son.

"Hopefully," she muttered, "my insurance company will see it that way, too, or I'm going to be making payments to Lucas until I'm eighty."

"No, you won't." He laid a few onions on top of the cheese bubbling atop the sizzling burgers in the smoke and steam. "I'll take care of that."

She stiffened at his presumption. It was one thing to accept Griffin's offer of a place to stay, but she wasn't about to let him pay for the kitchen rehab. "No, you won't. It's my kitchen, my house, my problem."

He frowned at her. "Don't be stubborn."

"Excuse me?"

"I mean it." He shrugged. "I can afford it. It's not like it'll kill me to handle the cost of the redo, Nicole."

This wasn't stubbornness, this was *pride,* and hers was taking a beating at the moment. Well, she might not have as much money as a King, but she could take care of her own problems.

"I'll kill you if you try," she said and waited until his gaze met hers again. "I don't care how much money you have, this is my responsibility. I can take care of myself, my son *and* my house."

He frowned at her. "Who the hell says you can't?"

"You just did," Nicole snapped, irritation blowing through her as fast as the electrical fire had moved through her kitchen. "Or implied it, anyway. I don't need to be rescued."

"Look around," he shot back. "I'm nobody's white knight."

"Not how it looks from where I'm standing."

"Yeah? Well, I don't see a horse and I'm not wearing armor."

No kidding, she thought grimly.

Nicole took another long breath, trying to steady herself. Griffin was just trying to help, she thought. Maybe it was the overblown, high-handed, arrogant kind of help the Kings so excelled at, but he wasn't *trying* to be offensive.

"Look," she said when she thought she could speak without either screaming or gritting her teeth, "I know you think you're doing the right thing by offering to step in and make everything okay again, but I can do this myself."

He studied her for a long moment and Nicole had to force herself to stand still under his steady stare. Finally, though, he said only, "Fine."

"Fine."

"Now that we've got that settled, why don't you get Connor and I'll bring the burgers to the table?"

He was giving in too easily, she told herself, even though his voice was tight and his eyes were grim. He wasn't happy about this, but Nicole told herself his happiness wasn't her issue. Griffin was just going to have to learn that not every woman in the world rolled over when a King spoke.

She'd been standing on her own two feet for a long time now and she wasn't about to let anyone—not even a well-meaning, would-be Knight in Shining Board Shorts—take control of what she did and didn't do.

She turned around sharply and left him standing there, staring after her. By the time she had Connor's hands washed and the boy secured in his booster seat, Griffin had already poured lemonade for all of them, including filling Connor's sippy cup. He handed it to the boy and smiled when Connor snatched it and sucked at the straw.

"Apparently moving dinosaurs through the desert is thirsty work," he said.

Relieved, Nicole smiled. Good, she was glad they'd left their previous conversation behind. Maybe he really was going to accept that *she* was in charge of what happened in her and her son's lives.

"Everything he does is thirsty work." She reached out and smoothed Connor's hair back from his forehead before breaking up a burger and laying a few bite-sized pieces on his tray.

"He's never still. Always interested in new things, that's Connor."

"All boys are like that, I think. At least, my brothers and I were," Griffin said, using a spatula to slide a burger onto her plate. "Our mom used to swear that one of us broke something every day."

She spooned potato salad onto Griffin's plate and then her own. "How many brothers do you have?"

He piled tomatoes onto his burger, added lettuce, then slapped the bun into place. Glancing at her, he smiled.

The power in that smile slammed into her and had Nicole's insides squirming.

"I thought you had all of us Kings figured out by now."

"I try, but you've got to admit, it's hard to keep track."

He laughed and something inside Nicole sizzled.

"Tell me about it. Hell—" He caught himself, glanced at Connor with a wince, then continued.

"None of us are sure how many of us there are but as for brothers...I've got five."

She blinked. "Seriously?"

Since she was an only child and her last living relative, her grandmother, had passed away several years ago, Nicole couldn't even imagine having that much family. And oh, a part of her really envied Griffin his brothers, his cousins, all of them. Most people thought about the Kings and the first thing that came to mind was their fortune, or the power they all seemed to wield so easily.

But Nicole had seen the Kings at family barbecues, at christenings and weddings, and she knew that they were much more than just the powerful Kings of California.

They were a family.

Griffin laughed. "Yeah. My dad always said that as soon as one of us started walking, our mom wanted another baby."

She looked at Connor and could totally understand. Nicole had wanted a lot of kids, too. But now it looked as though Connor would grow up as she had. An only child.

"But no matter how many of us there were and what we were into—football, baseball, basketball or scouts—Mom was always on top of things. We never could outwit her."

"You were a Boy Scout?"

Her tone must have conveyed her disbelief, because he straightened up as if insulted and said, "I was. Garrett and I went all the way to Eagle. If you need to know how to survive in the wilderness with a piece of string and a pocket-knife, just call us."

Nicole looked at him and tried to imagine him as a kid, but couldn't quite pull it off. His own fault, she thought, since he was far too overpowering as an adult to allow her to think of him as anything but an amazingly tempting man.

"Right. Eagle Scout. I'll remember."

He shrugged and took a bite of his burger. When he groaned in appreciation, that flutter inside her leaped into life again.

"Man," he said with reverence, "nothing beats a barbecued burger."

"Agreed."

His eyebrows went up. "We're *agreeing* on something? What's next? Friendship?"

She caught the teasing glint in his eye and fired right back, "Don't get your hopes up."

He slapped one hand to the center of his chest. "Shattered. You're a hard woman."

"Remember that."

"It's tattooed on my brain," he assured her.

She gave Connor more meat, then some potato salad and half a slice of tomato. The little boy dug right in.

"Lucas said once they get the rubble—" he winced a little, then continued "—cleared out, he'd be in touch with you about your choices for paint and flooring and all of the other stuff."

"Yeah, he told me in the email he sent with the estimate," Nicole said. With the conversation back to the kitchen, and with the thought of the cost whirling through her mind, she had to force herself to take a bite of the burger that moments ago had been delicious. Now it tasted like sawdust and threatened to get caught in her throat.

She chewed slowly, thoughtfully, and when she

swallowed she said, "I emailed him back and told him to just replace everything as it was."

"What?" Surprised, he asked, "You want linoleum again? That Formica countertop? Why not bring it up-to-date?" Then he must have realized why, because he nodded and muttered, "Right."

"Exactly," she said. "I can't afford to splurge on an upgrade. The wiring will be up-to-date and that's what matters. For right now, I'll just replace what I lost. Although I'm thinking that maybe I'll have them paint the walls a cool green instead of the pale yellow."

His mouth flattened into a grim line but he nodded.

If he thought she was happy about not updating the kitchen, he was wrong. Still, "In a few years, when I can, I'll build my dream kitchen."

"What'll it look like?" he asked, forking up some potato salad.

"Oh, it'll be gorgeous." Nicole closed her eyes briefly and saw her kitchen as she'd often imagined it. She'd had dreams of her own even before Rafe had redone Katie's kitchen. But seeing her friend's old, serviceable room transformed had fed her own dreams.

"I'd have wood floors," she mused aloud, "pale oak. I love that golden color. It's so warm."

"Yeah?"

"I'll keep the green walls to match that warmth with a splash of cool. Cupboards to match the flooring, of course," she said, seeing the kitchen so clearly in her mind's eye. "And the counters will be granite, but not that beige color everyone seems to choose or…ew…black."

He laughed and she looked at him. "What color?"

"Well, I love Katie's blue pearl, but for me, I'd get a dark cream color with streaks of green and blue running through it."

"Like green, do you?"

"Is there something wrong with green?"

"No way," he announced, waving his burger before he took another bite. "Go on, let's hear the rest."

"Pale-green walls, a stainless-steel sink, extra deep, with one of those gooseneck faucets like Katie has, of course…"

"Of course."

She eyed him. Was he laughing or just indulging her? Did it matter? Not to her.

"Stainless-steel appliances, too," she went on, seeing the huge new fridge she would one day indulge in, "and a six-burner stove—"

"Why so big? It's just you and Connor."

She shrugged. "I like to cook. And right now two of my burners don't work at all, so six sounds like heaven."

She gave Connor more of his hamburger. "Anyway, that's all in the distant future," she said, trying not to sound wistful. Fantasies were nice, but reality had to be faced. "For right now, I'll just be happy to have my own house back and the kitchen workable."

"Lucas will get it done. Fast and good."

"I know he will."

Pouring more lemonade for both of them, Griffin set the pitcher back down and said, "As for living here, don't worry about it. You and Connor are welcome. Like I told you, I'll stay out of your way and you just make yourself at home, okay?"

"I should be the one promising not to bug you. This is your vacation, right?"

"Yeah," he said with a short laugh. "Turns out, I'm not real good at the whole 'relaxation' thing. I was going buggy after the first three days."

"I don't know," she mused wryly, "you seem to enjoy spending time in the hot tub."

"What's not to enjoy?" He grinned and gave her a wink.

A quick jolt of heat shot through her, leaving trails of smoldering warmth in its wake.

"Besides," he said, "my assistant has already threatened to quit if I keep calling in to the office, so I'm forcing myself to stay in the water, away from the phone."

"You like working, don't you?"

"Guilty as charged," he admitted. "Garrett and I built King Security together. Well, after he sold his organics business to Chance."

She nodded. "King Organics."

"You got it."

"More expensive," she said, "but worth it."

"Naturally." Griffin gave her another wink and that fluttery feeling inside deepened. Honestly, the man was practically a walking orgasm. And Lord, it had been a long time since she'd had one of *those.*

"Anyway," Griffin was saying, "Garrett and I did nothing but the job for years, building the company. We breathed and slept the work. Then Garrett met Alex and…"

"He married a princess and moved to Cadria," Nicole finished for him.

"Exactly. So he's running the European branch and it's on me to keep the U.S. side running." He shrugged. "It's been busy and—"

"Weird without Garrett?" she asked. She knew Griffin and his twin were close. Having Garrett on the other side of the world must be hard.

"Yeah," he admitted. His mouth quirked. "Sounds dumb to say it out loud, but not having him around feels strange. Of course, if you repeat that, I'll deny it."

"Understood." She picked up her lemonade and took a sip. "Still, even with Garrett gone, you've got tons of family here."

"You could say that again," he mused. "Can't throw a rock in California without hitting a

King." He winked and gave her a wide smile. "I know. I've tried."

"I'll bet." Running her fingers up and down the sides of the icy-cold glass, Nicole said softly, "I've envied that. Such a big family. At the parties I've been to, you all seem to have so much fun when you're together."

"We do," he said. "So, you don't have a lot of family around here?"

She laughed a little. "Or anywhere else. My parents died when I was a kid and my grandparents went a few years ago." She turned her head to look across the fence at her place, now empty and burned, and she hoped her grandparents didn't know. Foolish, she thought, to worry about what they'd think of the accident, but her grandmother had loved that little kitchen. "They left me their house when they died."

As if sensing her thoughts, Griffin said, "It'll be back to normal in a couple of weeks, Nicole. Like the fire never happened."

She smiled, but all she could think was, it *had*

happened. And she knew it would be a long time before she would be able to forget what might have happened.

Four

Three days later, all Nicole could think was, thank God her laptop survived the fire.

With Connor at preschool, she was trying to catch up on work. She bent her head to the task of tallying up the billing for Comisky's flowers and told herself she was lucky in a lot of ways. She and Connor were both safe. The fire had been contained in the kitchen. She had insurance—okay, yes, with a huge deductible that was going to eat up her pitifully small savings and force her to maneuver a loan—but still. Her computer was safe, which meant she could keep working and making a living. And she and her son had a place to stay that wasn't costing them a fortune.

All good things.

The only downside...Griffin.

She stopped typing and sat back in her chair. Oh, he was trying to stay out of her way. She knew that. In the last three days, she'd only seen him at breakfast and at dinner. Otherwise, he was either in that damned hot tub or at the job site at her place or out in his car.

Probably best, she told herself firmly. Since the day he'd moved into Katie and Rafe's house, she'd been on edge. Desires she'd thought long dead had come back to life with a vengeance and she couldn't do anything with them.

Which had been making for some really annoying dreams.

In her dreams she felt Griffin's hands moving over her body and ached for more. Then she woke up miserable and had to face him over the breakfast table and pretend that she wasn't wondering just how good he was in bed.

Stupid.

He was probably *great.*

Didn't matter. She couldn't have an affair with Griffin. A, he wasn't interested and B...

Nicole stopped typing, closed the file she couldn't concentrate on and shut the lid of her laptop. There was a B, right? Of course there was a B. There had to be. But damned if she could think of what it was.

He was single—obviously. So was she. Okay, yes, she had Connor, but her son didn't really come into this equation. She wasn't looking for a husband and a father for Connor. All she was interested in was an actual orgasm. Or two. It had been *way* too long and Griffin was so...

For three nights she'd lain in her bed, knowing that Griffin was right across the hall, lying in his. For three nights she'd tossed and turned and then, when she finally did manage to fall asleep, there he was, starring in her dreams. Dreams that were hot enough to have her waking up needy and achy.

"How am I supposed to work when I can't stop thinking about him?" Naturally, she didn't have an answer to that question. Well, all right, she did know the answer, it just didn't help her. Honestly,

Nicole didn't know what to do. She was stuck here until her house was habitable again, and it was another two weeks before Rafe and Katie would come home. Which meant she and Griffin were going to stay in close quarters.

So she had to find a way to deal with the situation.

Right now, just like every day, Griffin was next door with his cousin and the crew he had working on her kitchen, though Nicole hadn't been back to her house since the first day the crew arrived. She'd stepped into the middle of controlled destruction and hadn't lasted long. Watching the guys take sledgehammers to the cupboards and what remained of the ceiling had just been too traumatic for her.

With every swing of their hammers, they were knocking down years of memories, and Nicole had vowed not to go back until the job was done. She trusted the Kings to do a good job, and having her underfoot wouldn't help anyway. So she worked with Lucas over the phone and by email and Griffin seemed determined to spend nearly every waking moment over there. Which was just one more good reason to avoid her own home.

Damn it. No matter what she did, her thoughts kept straying back to Griffin.

"This isn't working at all," she muttered and leaped up.

She grabbed her purse and car keys, then headed for the front door. What Nicole needed was some coffee and some common sense, not necessarily in that order. And since Katie was out of town, Nicole knew just where to go.

A half hour later, she was sitting at a small round table at Cupcake Central, owned by another of her clients and an old friend, Sandy Cannon.

"Your problem is, you're overthinking it," Sandy said, pausing for a sip of her latte. "I mean, he's gorgeous, so are you—"

Nicole laughed out loud at that one.

"—he's single and so are you. You're in the same house. What's the downside here?"

Frowning, Nicole looked at her friend. Sandy was married to her high school love, had three kids and ran a successful business. As far as Nicole could see, she pretty much had it all. Except, apparently, the power to talk Nicole out of doing something she really wanted to do.

"I came to you expecting to hear you say, *Stop. Don't. Run.*"

Sandy laughed. "Why would I say any of that? Do I look crazy?"

"Do I?" Nicole shook her head and stared down into her latte as if looking for help she wasn't finding anywhere else. "If I do this, it'll become a huge mess."

"How is good sex wrong?" Sandy asked, keeping her voice low so that none of her other customers would overhear.

"When it's with the absolutely *wrong* guy," Nicole answered.

"Okay," Sandy said, "tell me why he's so wrong for you."

"Where do I start?" Nicole snorted. "He's a King, for one thing."

"So? Most women in California are tripping over themselves trying to bump into one of the King men."

"Yeah, well, my best friend is married to one of them."

"And that's important because…"

"Because it might make things weird for Katie, and I don't want to do that."

"How would you having sex with one of Katie's cousins-in-law make life rough for her?"

"According to Griffin, she told all of the Kings that I was off-limits. She didn't want any of them hurting me."

Sandy frowned a little, broke off a piece of her raspberry cream-filled cupcake and popped it into her mouth. As she chewed, she said, "It's different if it's your idea."

"You think?"

"Absolutely."

"Still…" Oh, God, she was seriously considering jumping into bed with Griffin.

Sandy glanced over at the counter, where her employee was finessing an espresso machine into bursts of steam and hissing. When she looked back at Nicole, she leaned forward and lowered her voice. "It's been *years* since you've had sex."

Sighing, Nicole said, "You really don't have to remind me."

"Obviously I do, since it's right there in front of you and you're not grabbing hold—so to speak."

A wry smile curved Nicole's lips. "But Griffin is exactly the kind of man I swore I'd stay away from. He moves from woman to woman as easily as my ex-husband did."

"Which is why he's perfect," Sandy countered, a victorious smile on her face. "Seriously, girl, you're not looking for hearts and flowers here. You just want a little fun. What better guy to get it from? Think about it. No strings. No expectations. No promises to be broken…" She sat back in her chair. "Guys do it all the time. Why shouldn't we?"

All good points, Nicole acknowledged as her body began a slow burn in places that hadn't seen any kind of heat for way too long.

"It's a fling," Sandy said. "Like a summer vacation. God knows you could use a vacation. I've never seen anyone who works as much as you do—along with taking care of the house and Connor and—"

"I get it," Nicole said, cutting her friend off before she could really get going. "And Griffin is perfect."

"There you go!"

Could she do it? Could she have a quick, meaningless affair? She worried that thought in her mind for a minute or two. This so wasn't like her, but on the other hand...

This might be too good an opportunity to pass up.

"You know," she said, "I actually came here so you could talk me off the ledge, not give me a shove over."

"Please." Sandy grinned. "You never thought I'd talk you out of it. You were hoping I'd say go for it. And I am."

She had her there, Nicole admitted. Sandy had always been the go-for-the-brass-ring kind of girl. Of course she'd encourage Nicole to do exactly what she wanted to.

And, subconsciously at least, that's just what Nicole had wanted to hear.

When Sandy was called over to help at the counter, Nicole stayed where she was. Her gaze slid to the wide front window that overlooked Main Street. Crowds were thick during the summer. There were moms with kids, retired couples and streams of surfers headed toward the beach.

Seemed like everyone was enjoying their summer vacation. Except for her. Maybe Sandy was right. Maybe it was time Nicole did a little something for herself.

Nodding, she took another sip of her latte, ate the rest of her cupcake and made plans for seduction.

At least he was tired, Griffin thought, easing down into the hot tub. To keep busy today, he'd worked his ass off with Lucas's crew in Nicole's kitchen. He'd spent a few summers working construction as a kid, so he knew his way around a job site. Steve and Arturo had been happy for the help and, truthfully, Griffin had needed something to *do*. Something that would keep him out of the house and at a safe distance from Nicole. Something that would occupy him enough that his thoughts wouldn't have time to settle on the woman who was driving him nuts.

Now he was tired enough that he hoped for actual sleep tonight, and if he was really lucky, he wouldn't dream.

Because if he did, he knew Nicole would be the star in another *very* hot scenario that would have him waking hard and miserable.

"Good times," he muttered and laid his head back against the edge of the tub.

Overhead, the branches of the ancient elm waved and danced in the ocean breeze, making the leaves rattle gently. Glimpses of stars came and went between those branches and Griffin settled in to force himself to relax.

The old, settled neighborhood in Long Beach was quiet at night. Somewhere down the street, a dog barked and the muted sounds of rock music played in the air from someone's stereo. The whole scene was damn near perfect.

"Should be relaxing," he muttered, then he sat up and fisted his hands on the edges of the huge, square tub. Yeah. This wasn't working. Hell, he hadn't been anything but tense since he had started this vacation, no matter how many hours he tried to laze away in the hot tub he was beginning to hate.

"What's so great about a damn vacation anyway?" he whispered, his voice lost beneath the rush and rumble of the tub jets. "Why is work such a bad thing?"

There was no one to answer him—not that Griffin expected an argument. Hell, he knew that work was better than no work. Kept a man's mind occupied, increased his fortune and gave him something to *do*.

This whole mess was his own damn fault. He was the one who had decided to take some time. To rethink his workaholic, commitment-free lifestyle. Right about now, though, he wished to hell he was in his office buried in work. Or in Cadria visiting his twin. Or on a date with some nameless model. Hell, he wished he was on the other side of the planet, because since Nicole and Connor had moved in with him—

He shifted uncomfortably on the bench seat. Between the heat in his blood and the hot water pulsing around him, he was teetering on the edge of a very sharp cliff. All because he had wanted to change up his life. Mature.

Well, maturity was seriously overrated.

"You just have to hang on for a couple of weeks," he told himself in a whisper. "Lucas has an extra crew working on Nicole's place. It'll be done and she will be gone before you know it."

Perfectly reasonable.

It just didn't help him *now*.

Hell, nothing could. He was wound tight enough to give off sparks, for God's sake. And there was no end in sight. Thoughts blew through his mind, spinning with the force of a tornado. Griffin wasn't used to backing away from a beautiful woman. Turned out, it was damned uncomfortable.

He thunked the back of his head against the edge of the tub. "You could just leave the house to Nicole and her son and go to a hotel. Hell, screw the whole vacation thing and go back to work, too."

But that thought hit him wrong. Not only would his twin never let him forget it if Griffin gave up early and went back to work, but leaving the house now would be like running away, and one thing a King *never* did was turn tail and run. They stood their ground, even when that ground was crumbling beneath their feet, dropping them into an abyss of misery and pain.

He snorted. "Do-it-the-hard-way-Kings. That's us."

"Talking to yourself again?"

He sat up straight, sending water sloshing against the rim of the hot tub. Turning his head, he watched as Nicole stepped out of the house and walked toward him. Immediately he wished he hadn't looked at her at all.

Damn.

He'd known the woman had a great body, but admiring her curves under a layer of tank tops and shorts was different than seeing those same curves defined by a bikini small enough to barely merit being called a swimsuit.

In the wash of moonlight, her skin gleamed like warm honey and looked just as smooth. Her breasts were perfect, high and full and just barely hidden by the triangles of neon-green material. Her belly was flat, her hips rounded, and as his eyes were drawn down to another scrap of fabric at the juncture of her thighs, his own body went hard as stone.

Oh, man. This was not a good thing.

"Wow," she murmured, tipping her head and smiling at him. "Didn't think I'd ever see Griffin King suddenly struck speechless."

He scrubbed one hand across his face and shook his head. Damned if he'd give Nicole the upper hand in this. No woman had ever knocked him on his ass before, and he wasn't about to let this be the first time. He couldn't afford to have a clouded mind—especially not now. Though how he was supposed to think about anything but the body she was displaying, Griffin didn't know.

"Yeah. Sorry. Didn't hear you come out here." He looked past her and frowned. "Where's Connor?"

"In bed," Nicole said and handed over a bottle of wine and two glasses that he hadn't even noticed she was carrying.

Watch your step, Griffin, he warned himself.

That warning went right out the window as he watched her mount the steps and slide slowly into the tub. She settled on the bench seat right beside him and Griffin would have sworn that the water temperature went up another hundred degrees.

"Oh, that feels good." Her voice was a purr of pleasure that sent jagged bolts of need shooting through his body.

Danger.

"What're you doing?" Hell, she'd been alternately snarling at him and ignoring him for days. All of a sudden she showed up, barely dressed, carrying wine? Something was definitely up— besides *him*. Griffin shifted uncomfortably and inched a bit farther away from the temptation right beside him.

He wasn't an idiot. If she was here, she had something more than relaxing in the hot tub in mind. And damned if he was going to let his hormones take control until he knew exactly what was running through her brain.

She turned her head and smiled at him. Something in his chest caught and held in response.

"Thought I'd see for myself just why you spend so much time in this hot tub." One of the jets bubbled and frothed at her back and she sighed again. "I think I get it."

As she arched into the jet, her breasts rose above the surface of the water and he stifled a groan. "Great. Happy to help. Now…"

"I brought wine," she said, and nodded toward the open bottle he held.

"Yeah, I see that, but—"

"I've got the baby monitor out here, too. Sitting on the table by the back door. If Connor needs me, I'll hear him." She shrugged and took the acrylic wineglasses from him, holding both out for him to fill. "So, how about you pour the wine and we'll just sit and enjoy for a while?"

He could use a drink. On the other hand, he thought, drinking wine with a beautiful woman while in a hot tub was only going to lead in one direction.

He smiled to himself.

Damn, even when he knew better, he couldn't resist the lure she was holding out in front of him.

"So?" Nicole waved both empty glasses. "Are you going to pour, or would you rather I leave?"

There was his out. He should grab it with both

hands. Instead, he poured the wine. He wasn't letting her go anywhere until he knew what she was up to. This whole setup—alone in the darkness, wine, hot tub—was an ambush, and a damned good one. If he slipped out of her clutches now, without knowing what was going on, she'd just trip him up somewhere else along the line. Better to be prepared.

Reaching over the edge of the tub, he set the bottle down on the top step, then settled back, took a long drink of the wine and speared her gaze with his. "So, you want to tell me what's going on, Nicole?"

"Not sure what you mean," she said, a small smile curving her mouth as she sipped at her wine.

Women. He was pretty sure they were born knowing just how to twist a man into knots. And not to knock his own gender, but Griffin was willing to admit, at least silently, that it wasn't difficult for them at all. Show a man a beautiful woman and he was already on a slippery slope. Give him one of those sexy half smiles and his fall started picking up speed.

"You know just what I mean." Her smile deepened, and she slid a glance at him from the corners of her eyes. She was definitely up to something. And in Griffin's experience, when a woman had a plan, every man in the vicinity should be on guard. "You've never joined me out here before. Why now? Why the wine?"

"Look," she said simply, "it's a nice night. I've had a long day, and the hot tub sounded like a great idea." Shrugging, she pointed out, "You must like it. You're in it every day."

Lately to avoid being with her, Griffin thought, though now he could see the flaw in that strategy. At least if they were in the living room watching TV she'd be *dressed*.

The image of her in that bikini flashed across his already fevered brain. Then his gaze dropped to the surface of the churning water that bubbled and frothed at the tops of her breasts. Oh, man.

"Something wrong?"

"Nope. Nothing." He shifted on the bench seat and ordered his body to throttle back. Unfortunately, that particular portion of him had its own ideas. And they had nothing to do with cooling off.

Didn't matter. He was still in control.

"Good," Nicole said, then paused for another long sip of wine. When she'd swallowed, she turned her head to look at him. "Because there's something I want to talk to you about."

And here it comes. Finally. "Yeah? What's that?"

"I want to have a night with you."

The long drink of wine he'd taken logjammed in the middle of his throat and Griffin choked in response. Whatever he'd been expecting, it hadn't been *this*. Nicole Baxter propositioning *him?* What kind of crazy-ass world had he been dropped into?

When he could breathe again, he stared at her. "Are you serious?"

She scooted closer. "Absolutely."

Griffin held his ground. Even though he knew he should back away while he still could, he couldn't quite bring himself to do it.

"I know you're interested," Nicole was saying

and he silently warned himself to listen up. "I've seen the way you look at me, Griffin."

He cleared his throat. So much for his poker face. "No offense, but that just means I'm alive and breathing, Nicole."

She smiled again, as if she knew that was a weak argument.

"You've been avoiding me," she said.

Damn straight he had, not that he was going to admit it.

"Giving you space," he argued.

"Hiding," she countered.

Okay, that wasn't acceptable. "I don't hide."

"Then why do you look nervous?"

Griffin laughed shortly. "Babe, I haven't been nervous around a woman since I was fifteen."

"Until now," she said, taking another sip of wine.

Griffin gritted his teeth. He wasn't nervous. He was…*cautious*. There was a difference. Any man would be cautious walking through a minefield.

"What're you getting at here, Nicole?"

"I already told you," she said with another

shrug that briefly lifted the tops of her breasts. "I think we should have a fling."

His mouth went dry. He hadn't seen this coming at all. Which explained, he told himself, why he couldn't seem to string a coherent sentence together. Finally he managed one word.

"Because?"

"Because you want me. I want you. There's no reason *not* to."

He really was in the twilight zone, because he was pretty sure he'd used that same argument with other women at other times. Odd having his own words thrown back at him.

But as tempted as he was, by her presence, her idea, there was one thing he couldn't forget. "You have a son."

"Connor's not a part of this."

He nodded toward the baby monitor. "Yeah. He is. And I have rules about that."

"*Rules?* What kind of rules?"

"The kind that means I don't get involved with women who have kids." Memories rose up, but Griffin ruthlessly shut them down. This wasn't about his past. This was about now.

"We wouldn't be involved," she corrected. "We'd be having sex."

Griffin laughed shortly again. "That's involved. Trust me."

"Doesn't have to be." Nicole scooted even closer and now her thigh brushed against his, stirring into roaring life the deeply stifled hunger he'd been dealing with.

"I'm not looking for a relationship, Griffin," she told him sharply, "so don't make this so complicated. I just want a damn orgasm or two."

"I can't believe we're having this conversation," he said, muffling a laugh.

"Why shouldn't we talk about this?" she argued. "Have you never had a woman come on to you before?"

"Of course I have, but this is dif—"

"How is it different?" Her blue eyes glinted with more than passion now. There was anger there as well, and damned if that didn't intrigue him, too.

She started talking again before he could say a word.

"I've been divorced three years. You know how long it's been since I had sex?"

He stared into her flashing eyes and didn't think he could have looked away if someone had a gun to his head. Those soft eyes of hers were burning with a fire he understood. And shared.

"How long?"

"Three years," she said shortly. She took a deep breath. "When my husband first left me, I was too hurt and furious to even so much as *think* about sex. The second year, I was just too busy— what with work and Connor and... Anyway, now it's been three years and I'm *ready*. Boy, am I ready."

He was getting more ready by the second, so he could agree. "Yeah, I get that."

"Good." She nodded, took a breath and blew it out again. "Look, Griffin, I know your reputation."

"Is that right?"

"I'm not an idiot, you know. I see your picture in magazines and newspapers, and I do live right next door to Katie. She keeps me up-to-date on what the Kings are up to. So," she continued, "I know you're a player—different-woman-every-night kind of guy—"

"Hey—" Griffin started to argue, but what the hell could he say? He *was* that guy. At least, he *had* been until he'd made the decision to grow the hell up. For all the good that was doing him.

"No offense," she said quickly. "In this case, your inability to commit is a plus."

"My—"

"Seriously, you're not interested in forever and trust me when I say I'm not, either, Griffin. I just want one good night. A damn fling. And you are *so* flingable."

He snorted.

"As long as you're healthy—" She stopped. "You *are* healthy, right?"

"Of course I am."

She blew out a breath. "Okay, good. Great, in fact."

Griffin could only stare at her. This was the weirdest situation he'd ever been in. He'd never had a woman come to him with an offer like this one. He'd always been the pursuer, not the pursued, and frankly, he was a hell of a lot more comfortable when he was calling the shots.

Still, he thought resignedly, there was something to be said for variety, right?

Five

"You're crazy, you know that, right?"

"What's your point?" she asked, one corner of her mouth curving.

Griffin smiled and reached for her. "Guess I don't have one."

This will be good, he told himself as he plucked her wineglass from her hand and set both glasses on the step. Get her into bed and get over it. Once he'd had her, Nicole would be like every other woman he'd ever met. She'd stop taunting his every damn thought and he'd be able to sleep in peace again. Then they could both move on.

Hell, this was brilliant.

He should have come up with this idea himself, and if she hadn't been making him so nuts lately, he might have. But, he told himself, he wouldn't have made a move on her anyway. Not with the single-mother thing. Not to mention the fact that his cousin's wife would *kill* Griffin if he hurt Nicole.

Well, hell, what was a little threat of death when compared to a completely alluring woman in a tiny bikini?

"No strings," she whispered.

"No promises," he agreed.

"Just a fling."

"Absolutely."

"I brought condoms." She pulled a few foil packets from where she'd stashed them beneath the ties at the side of her bikini.

"Good thinking," Griffin murmured just before he took her mouth in a kiss he'd been thinking about for days.

The first touch of her lips was electric. The sensation sizzled through him like a live wire dropped onto wet pavement. He was on fire. Every cell in his body shouted hallelujah.

He parted her lips with his tongue and she opened for him willingly, eagerly. Her tongue tangled with his, shooting fresh need through his system. He dragged her closer, pulling her onto his lap, bending her back over his arm, his mouth locked to hers. Her arms came up around his neck, her hands sliding over his warm, wet skin.

The glide of her fingers against his back was frantic, as if she couldn't touch him enough, and Griffin felt the same. He held her tighter, closer, and still he wanted more of her. Her body was slender yet curvy in all the right places and he wanted to explore them all.

He slid one hand to cup her right breast and she arched into him. His thumb brushed across her hardened nipple and she shuddered.

"Griffin!"

"Oh, yeah," he whispered, drawing back to look down at her. Her eyes were glazed, her mouth parted on a sigh of pleasure as his fingers continued to tug and toy with her nipples, one after the other.

She wiggled on his lap and he hissed in reaction. He was as hard as stone and so tight he felt as if he might explode with one wrong move.

So he was going to make all of the right ones.

He took hold of her waist, drew her up and set her across him, straddling his lap. Damn near killed him, but he maintained. Her knees on the bench seat, she leaned in toward him and smiled as her breasts brushed across his chest. "This is great. Really."

"It's about to get better," he promised in a hushed tone barely audible over the roar of the jets.

"Show me."

"Just about to," he said and kissed her again. God, the taste of her, he thought, losing himself in the sensations pouring through him. The feel of her in his arms. Her legs pressed to his. Her breath sifting into his mouth. Griffin was nearly blind with lust. He'd never wanted any other woman so much. Never had been so dazzled by the taste of any woman that he was like a man dying for more.

And though a warning chime went off somewhere in the back of his mind, Griffin ignored it. Whatever was going on between them was a worry for some other time. All he wanted, *needed* now was to be inside her. To claim her body as thoroughly as he'd dreamed of doing.

He slid his hands to the sides of her bikini bottoms and tugged. Following his lead, she went up on her knees and slithered out of the fabric as he drew it down her legs. By the time she was free of them, she was nearly breathless. So was Griffin.

"Touch me."

"Plan to," he assured her and cupped the core of her.

She groaned, a deep, throaty sound that seemed to reach for the center of his chest and squeeze. Hunger radiated through him, and yet there was more than his own need gnawing at him. There was the need to watch her orgasm. To feel release ripple through her body. To see the flash of satisfaction gleam in her eyes.

He slid one finger inside her and smiled when she gasped again.

"That feels so good…"

"Gonna be better," he said and dipped two

fingers into her heat, pushing them high, stroking, caressing the depths of her body until she was trembling and swaying on her knees. He wrapped one arm around her back to hold her still and used his fingers to drive her wild. His touch claimed her in swift, sure strokes as his thumb caressed that one sensitive nub of flesh at her center until she clutched at his shoulders for balance. She threw her head back and her blond hair swung in a wide arc behind her as she gave herself up entirely to the feelings he was causing.

His gaze locked on her, his own body clamored for release, but he was caught up in what she was feeling. His heartbeat thundered, his mouth went dry and as he gently pushed her over the edge, he held her safely in his arms.

Nicole could hardly breathe and wasn't sure if she cared or not. All she could think of was the dazzling pleasure she'd just found. It had been so long since a man had touched her, and even then, she was forced to admit, it had been nothing like *this*.

She looked into Griffin's summer-blue eyes and

read the passion she'd longed for. That she'd come
to him to find. She still couldn't believe she'd had
the guts to lay out this proposition to him, but
she was so glad she had. The fire, the heat she
saw in his eyes was something she wanted now
more than ever.

Her hands slid across his shoulders, slick with
water, and she felt the taut muscles beneath his
skin. His hair was as black as midnight and the
light in his eyes shone just for her. For this one
moment, anyway, Nicole was the only woman
in Griffin King's life, and that thought spiraled
through her mind and body like a straight shot
of warm tequila.

The hot water lapped at her body as he lowered her to his lap. She felt the hard length of him
pressed against her still-quivering core and the
fire inside her jumped into life again. This was
the *best* night ever.

"That was so good," she said, leaning forward
to plant a quick kiss on his mouth. He caught her
there and deepened the kiss, dragging it out until
her head swam and her blood boiled. The sweep
of his tongue against hers, the feel of his breath

sliding into her lungs, the touch of his hands at her back, it was all sensation overload.

She was melting against him, folding into that broad, sculpted chest she'd been sneaking peeks of for so long. When he finally released her, he slid his hands to the front clasp of her bikini top. "Only the beginning," he said.

"I am so glad to hear that," Nicole whispered and shrugged out of her top. He tossed it over the edge of the tub and she instantly felt more... wicked. Naked in a hot tub with Griffin King. The kind of thing dreams were made of, she thought absently as his hands moved to cup her breasts.

Then every thought in her head cut off completely. How could she think when Griffin was touching her? She sighed and didn't bother trying to hide her reaction. "You have magic hands."

"So I've been told."

"I'll bet you have," she said. And if a warning bell sounded in her mind, she ignored it. She had known going in that he was a player. That a lot of women had been where she was now. Oh, all right, not in this particular hot tub, but with *him*. Feeling what he was doing to her.

But tonight, she didn't care about how many women he'd been with. The point was, he was with her *now*. That was all that mattered. One night. One week. She didn't care how long it lasted. This was *her* fling and she was going to enjoy every minute of it.

"This was the best idea I've ever had," Nicole said softly, and meant it. No matter what happened after tonight, she wouldn't regret anything.

"Have to agree," Griffin told her.

Warm water bubbled and frothed around them. The jets pulsed like a quickening heartbeat in the darkness. Nicole savored the feel of the water caressing her skin even as Griffin's hands moved up and down her back. He leaned in and kissed the line of her throat and she tipped her head to one side, allowing him more room. His hands fell to her waist and with one smooth move, he lifted her off him.

"Hey—"

"One second—" In what seemed like less than that, he'd stripped off his board shorts, stood up to sheath himself in one of the condoms she'd provided and reached for her again. He positioned her exactly the way she had been and this time when Nicole lowered herself onto his lap, there was no swimsuit between them. All she felt was *him*. She sucked in a gulp of air and met his gaze squarely.

"Gotta have you," Griffin said, holding her hips in a firm grip.

"Oh, me, too." Nicole raised up and then, still keeping her eyes on his, lowered herself again, this time taking him inside her. Inch by glorious inch, he filled her, and Nicole's body stretched to accommodate him. It had been so long since she'd been with anyone, it was as if it was the first time.

Only better.

"Oh, yeah," he whispered and pushed himself even deeper inside.

Nicole gasped and wriggled her hips, creating a delicious friction that only made the ache she was feeling sweeter, more desperate.

"You're gonna kill me if you keep that up," he warned.

"You want me to stop it then," she asked, tossing her hair back from her face.

"God, no," he countered quickly. "Never stop. I'll risk death. It'd be worth it."

"Just what I was thinking," she admitted and began to move on him.

His hands at her hips guided her and still she couldn't move fast enough. She needed… needed…

"That's it," Griffin muttered and shifted. Keeping their bodies locked together, he twisted around until Nicole was reclined on the narrow bench seat and he was looming over her.

"I need you bad," he confessed and Nicole read the truth in his eyes. He was as inflamed as she. As lost to the amazing sensations. Need was alive and tearing at them both. Hunger roared around them and they answered.

She slapped one hand onto the lip of the hot tub and held tight as Griffin moved on her. He withdrew and then plunged even deeper than before and she groaned even as her hips lifted to meet his. Again and again, he pistoned against her, his hands firmly gripping her thighs, holding her in place while his body claimed hers.

The orgasm he'd given her earlier was nothing compared to what was coming. She felt tension clawing at her. Felt her release hovering just out of reach. She worked for it. Sliding her free hand over his chest and around to his broad, slick back. The feel of him under her hands was nearly as sexy as the feel of his body sliding deep.

Her breath shortened, her heartbeat thundered and the friction within sizzled.

"Griffin!"

"Go," he urged, his voice a rasp of urgency. "Let go, Nicole."

"With you," she said, just as desperately, feeling her climax begin to crash down on her. "Both of us."

He laughed harshly. "Stubborn woman."

"Oh, yeah," she agreed, then clutched his behind and pulled him tightly to her just as they exploded together and rode that flash of heat as it consumed them.

A few minutes later, they were sprawled in the hot tub, grinning at each other, and Griffin realized he'd never enjoyed himself with a woman as much as he just had. Fling or not, there was more of a connection with Nicole than he'd ever had before, too.

They'd been friends first, he thought and maybe that was the difference. The question was, now that they'd had each other, would they still be friends?

"That was…" Nicole said, floating lazily in the water.

"Yeah, it really was," Griffin told her, reaching out to stroke one hand along the length of her body.

She shivered. And turned her head to look at him. "Oh, now you're just teasing me."

"Just keeping you in the mood."

"No worries there," she said on a sigh, "the way I feel right now…"

"Now who's teasing?" he asked and grabbed her ankle to pull her closer.

She wrapped one arm around his neck and slid her free hand down across his chest. "I can see why you like this hot tub so much. It's great," she said.

"It is *now*," he told her and caught her hand

in his. Her fingers were long, slender. Her eyes were swimming with the glaze of spent passion and banked fires.

He could hardly believe what had just happened. He'd known Nicole for more than a year, and yet now, it was all different. Of course...

He chuckled. "Y'know, if Katie ever hears about this, she'll kill me."

"Oh," Nicole said lightly, "Katie won't find out from me. I don't want *anyone* to know."

He just looked at her. Griffin didn't know if he was excited by a secret affair or insulted that she was so determined to keep him hidden.

"I mean, really," Nicole continued, leaning into him, "I'm in no hurry to tell people that I blackmailed a man into a night of sex, which I completely did—because you *so* owed me for the kitchen."

That was something, he supposed. Not that she was trying to hide him so much as she was trying to avoid mention of blackmail. Then he asked, "So have I paid my debt?"

"It's a good down payment," she told him with a smile.

"Yeah?" He grinned at her. "Well, it *was* a hell of a fire."

"Exactly. Might take a little while to settle up."

"I'm a man who pays my debts," he told her.

"Glad to hear it."

He sensed that she was ready for more, and God knew he was. He couldn't remember any other time when he'd been this hungry for a woman. When just the brush of her hand against his skin was damn near molten.

No, there'd never been another like Nicole. And when he was capable of rational thought again, he'd have to spend some time considering what that might mean. But for now...

"Come here," he whispered and met her halfway. His mouth was just a breath away from hers when it happened.

"Mommmmmmmyyyyy..."

A warbling voice erupted from the baby monitor and they both turned to look at it. Just like that, the spell between them shattered. Hearing Connor's voice was like a cold shower for Griffin, and he guessed the same was true for Nicole. She pulled back and reached for the monitor, turning down the volume. Connor's cries were muffled now, but no less insistent.

"Guess our night is over," she said, reluctance obvious in her tone. "I've got to go."

"Yeah, I know." He lifted one hand and smoothed a wet lock of her hair back from her face, trailing his fingertips across her cheek as he did.

One touch.

He was on fire again with no hope of quenching it. One damn night. It might have been enough with anyone else, but with Nicole...

Connor's voice reached for them from inside the house, reminding each of them that their night was over. That reality had come crashing down on them.

"You'd better go," Griffin said quietly. He wanted to grab hold of her and keep her just where she was. But he couldn't and he knew it. Didn't make letting her go any easier, though.

She closed her eyes briefly. "Sorry this had to end so soon."

"Yeah, me, too."

"Is it...weird between us now?"

"Getting there," he said softly. They were talking to each other like polite strangers when only minutes before he'd had his mouth on her breasts and her long, lovely legs wrapped around his waist. Yeah. It was weird.

Connor's voice had shattered the moment between them and it was probably good that it had. Sex was simple. This situation with Nicole wasn't. Best to remember that.

She nodded. "I thought it might be hard between us…after."

Sure it would be, Griffin thought. Every time he looked at her now, he'd remember and want more. "Not gonna be the way it was, that's for sure."

"It was still worth it," she told him.

"Oh, it really was."

Smiling, she started to climb out of the tub, then stopped, sank lower into the water and looked at him. "This is going to sound ridiculous, but would you close your eyes?"

"Seriously?" He smiled in spite of the tension coiled in the pit of his stomach. "I've seen every inch of you."

"Yeah, but that—" she waved one hand at the water, vaguely indicating what they'd just been doing "—was different."

"You keep surprising me."

"A good thing, right?"

"Yeah, I guess it is. You know," he said, snaking out one hand to grab up her bikini, "you could just put these back on."

"Takes too long to try to wiggle back into them in the water. Griffin, come on. Close your eyes for a second so I can go to Connor."

Like nobody else, he told himself. Nicole was completely unique. How she could be shy or embarrassed after what they'd just shared was beyond him, but he was intrigued by her more and more. She was a complicated woman, he thought, smiling to himself. She didn't react to anything the way he expected her to. She wasn't easy to read and he found that exciting. Hell, Griffin had known how to deal with every woman he'd ever known, until Nicole. She kept him off balance, though—off his game—and, he thought, that might not be a plus in the long run.

"Fine," he said finally and closed his eyes on that last, disturbing thought.

"Thanks." He heard the water slosh and her feet as she stepped onto the top level of the stairs. "I'm going to grab your towel, too, since I forgot to bring one."

"No problem." His eyes were still closed, but his imagination worked just fine. In his mind, he saw her wrap the towel around her body. He saw rivulets of water running down her arms and legs and sliding down the curve of her throat and everything in him yearned to lick them all off.

"Okay," she said, "I'm good."

Griffin opened his eyes again and found reality even better than his imagination. She looked warm and wet and completely amazing draped only in a white towel. She watched him through blue eyes that still held a trace of passion, and damned if he didn't want to grab her and pull her back down into the hot tub.

So much for worrying about being off-balance, he thought wryly. At the moment, he didn't give a damn what she was doing to his equilibrium—he just wanted her.

But playtime was over and she was clearly moving into Mommy mode.

"So," she said, inching closer to the back door, "this was great, and I'll, uh, see you tomorrow, right?"

"Right."

He stared after her for a long minute even after the door was closed and he was alone. She'd wanted one night. But now he wanted more.

That realization told him two things.

He was walking on dangerous ground—and he had no intention of turning back.

The downside to Connor getting older was the advent of nightmares.

Nicole tucked the blanket around her son, then smoothed one hand across his baby-soft blond hair. He was curled up on one side, hugging his stuffed alligator to his tiny chest. She had held him and soothed him and then settled him down again. Now, with his trusted buddy cuddled in tight, Connor slipped back into sleep, whatever nightmare had awakened him already forgotten.

Moonlight slid through the windows of Con-

nor's borrowed room. Most of his things were
still at their house, but Griffin had made it a point
to bring over enough of Connor's toys to make
the boy feel more comfortable—a gesture that
had both surprised and touched Nicole. He wasn't
who she'd expected him to be. Who would have
thought that Griffin would realize how important
familiarity would be to a two year old? Having
his things around him had made the transition
to this temporary move a lot easier on Connor.

She glanced around at a few of the books he
loved to "read." The toy cars at the foot of his
bed and the chalkboard in the corner. Treasures
that made up the center of Connor's world. Just
as her son made up the center of Nicole's world.

She shifted her gaze to her little boy. He looked
so small, lying in the wide double bed that had
been pushed up against a wall. She had piled pil-
lows on one side of him so he wouldn't roll off, but
that only served to make him look even smaller
than he was. But she smiled, remembering how
excited Connor had been to be given a "big-boy
bed." He was growing up right in front of her.

How fast it had all gone, she thought.

The quiet settled around her and she walked to the window, staring down at the street that was as familiar to her as her own name. The neighborhood in Long Beach was old and settled, with bungalows tucked back from the street and yards filled with big trees that shaded the road in summer in what looked like a long, green arch. Families lived here. It was safe. Quiet. And Nicole loved everything about it.

She'd run here, run *home,* when her husband left her. There had been renters in her grandmother's house then, but she'd broken the lease and moved in herself. Being in that house, with the memories of love surrounding her, had grounded her when she'd most needed it. Being on this street where she knew everyone had soothed raw nerves and helped her find her way again.

Then she and Katie had gotten close and that had helped Nicole remember who she really was. She'd found the strength to face the fears of being alone and pregnant. She'd let go of the fury she'd felt toward the husband who had deserted her when she needed him most and realized that being on her own was better than being with the wrong person.

Then Connor had been born, and from that moment, she'd been nothing but grateful. The last few years hadn't been easy, being both mom and dad and scrambling for clients to help grow her business. But she wouldn't change any of it. She'd become stronger than she had ever thought she could be. And she had Connor. That was enough.

At least it *had* been.

Now, after only one shattering experience with Griffin, Nicole wondered if there might be more for her out there somewhere. Oh, not with Griffin, obviously. He wasn't the staying kind of guy, which was exactly why she'd come up with this whole night-of-wahoo idea in the first place. Although he was really sweet with Connor.

"And," she whispered, "he's fun to be with, to talk to, to argue with. And he *really* looks good and wow, what that man can do to a woman—"

Stop it! Her mind shouted at her, dragging her back from fantasy to reality with a crashing jerk. Right. She was a mom, he was a player and never the twain should meet. Well, probably shouldn't meet again, anyway.

Sighing softly, she glanced at her son again, then quietly walked across the room and checked the night-light before slipping out the door into the hall. A few steps later, she was in her own room.

She set the baby monitor on the bedside table and looked out the window into the backyard. She couldn't see the hot tub from here, but her mind provided the image she was interested in: Griffin, sprawled in that hot water, eyes still hazy with passion, body still primed for more.

A tingling sensation opened up inside her, low and deep and achy. Nicole sighed, relishing that feeling even as she worried about it. She should have been satisfied with what had happened earlier. She'd needed an orgasm and boy howdy, had she gotten one. Well, two. That didn't mean she'd be getting more of the same. This was supposed to be a one-night thing. A moment's excitement. A simple release of tension. Have sex with Griffin, then go back to the way things had been.

But it felt like more than that, and she didn't know what to do about it.

What she really needed to do was talk to her best friend about all of this.

She turned away from the window, flopped back onto the bed and stared blindly at the ceiling. "Idiot," she muttered. "You can't call Katie. You don't want Katie to even know what you did with Griffin, remember? You can't call her."

And it was pointless to talk to Sandy again. She already knew what that friend would have to say—"Go for it!"

But she couldn't. Could she?

Her door opened and her heart jumped. She turned her head to see Griffin, standing in the doorway. He was still wearing his bathing suit. But then, she was still draped in a towel.

"Connor okay?"

"He's fine. Just a nightmare." Silly to be nervous. Almost as silly as having him close his eyes when she got out of the tub. But it had been a long time since she'd done anything like this, and Nicole felt a little on edge. What was she supposed to do here? Welcome him inside? Tell him to go away? Drop her towel and ask for more of what she'd already had?

Okay, that's the one she wanted to do.

So, deliberately, she sat up and tucked the end of the towel more firmly into the drape between her breasts. "He went right back to sleep."

"Good." He walked into the room, and closed the door behind him. "That's good." He stood there, back to the door, and watched her.

Tension sizzled in the room between them and Nicole could have sworn that every breath singed her lungs.

"I wanted to talk to you," Griffin said, his voice a low rumble.

"Okay...about what?" Oh, God, don't let it be something like, *You're a nice woman but, seriously, the sex wasn't that good and you should probably think about joining a convent.*

"I'm not done," he blurted.

"What?" Heat shot through her.

He shoved one hand through his hair, then scrubbed that hand across the back of his neck. "I'm not done. With you."

Six

Nicole's breath came short and fast. Her gaze was locked on the man staring at her as if she were a banquet and he was coming off a long fast.

"The thing is," he grumbled, "you came to me. You wanted one night."

"I remember," she said.

"Now I'm coming to you." Griffin braced his bare feet wide apart and folded his arms over his really fabulously sculpted, broad chest. "And I want more than one night. Do you?"

Here was her chance. To stick to the plan. To relish the orgasms she'd had and let the promise of future ones slide away. Return to normal. Return to the way things had been between them and try to pretend nothing had changed.

Problem was, she didn't want to do any of that. What she wanted was Griffin.

"Yes," she said, swallowing hard, loving the swirl of nervous expectation that was suddenly flooding her. "I'm not done with you, either."

He gave her a fast smile that lit up his eyes and did some pretty amazing things to her body, too. That sense of expectation was skyrocketing, and the tingling sensation at her core was practically vibrating.

"Okay then." He walked toward her in long, slow steps. "New rules. We let this play out until we're both finished. Or until you move back to your place."

Funny, just yesterday, she'd been thinking how anxious she was for things to get back to normal. Now, not so much. As for the other thing, she didn't want to think about being finished. She wanted, right now, to grab hold of Griffin and feel again what he'd made her feel just a little while ago. Now that she'd had a taste of what she could find with Griffin, she was greedy and not ashamed to admit it—at least to herself. Her body was coming back to life with a vengeance.

"That sound good to you?"

Beyond good. Because he was there, watching her, with hunger in his eyes.

"Sounds great." She reached up for him as he leaned over her. "But Griffin, I still don't want anyone to know. That's still part of the deal."

"Agreed." He didn't look as though he enjoyed saying that, but he had and that was what mattered.

If they were going to have a real affair rather than a one-night stand, then it was more important than ever that no one know about this. Because eventually it would be over and she really didn't want sympathy from people when Griffin went back to his real life, leaving her behind.

Just the thought of that was enough to steel her spine. "So in public," she said, "we behave just like we always have."

"You mean argue and snipe?" he asked, a small smile curving his mouth. Honestly, Nicole had never seen a better weapon to use on a woman than that soft, secretive smile. "Shouldn't be hard to remember to argue."

Wryly, she said, "True."

"But in private," he whispered, leaning down over her, planting both hands on the bed, caging her between his arms.

"In private…" Caught in his eyes, Nicole swallowed hard and licked suddenly dry lips.

"We have each other as often as possible," he said softly, dipping his head to claim a fast, hard kiss.

"Oh, yeah, that sounds fabulous." Nicole reached up to cup his face between her palms.

"See?" he said. "No argument. You have more of those condoms handy?"

She nodded. "Bedside table drawer."

He tugged the drawer open, grabbed a condom and ripped it open. Quickly, he stripped out of his suit and sheathed himself. When he was protected, he turned back to her, plucked the knot of her towel free, pulled the fabric off her and tossed it aside before laying her back on the bed. Nicole looked up at him. The moonlight glimmered on his skin, his hair, and shone in his eyes. Her heartbeat jumped into a gallop and every nerve in her body flared into life.

Griffin dipped his head to take first one of her hardened nipples into his mouth and then the other. And with each lick of his tongue, each tugging draw from his lips, she felt herself coming to life again. Heat bubbled inside her and that oh, so delicious swirl of something amazing settled in the pit of her stomach and then slid lower.

Her skin was bristling for his touch. Moonlight caressed his skin just as she wanted to. Her hands smoothed across his chest and over his shoulders, then down his arms. Then he covered her body with his. Skin met skin, mouth claimed mouth. Hands explored, grasped, held. Legs entwined and bodies arched. Breath huffed into the air on short, sharp gasps filled with need and desperation.

Everything Nicole had felt earlier came back in a rush and was magnified. The quilt beneath her was cool, Griffin's body was hot and hard and oh, so perfect.

She parted her legs for him and watched him as he took her, pushing his body slowly into hers.

His features tightened into a mask of need and pleasure. She lifted her hips, taking him deeper, higher. He filled her so completely, she felt as though he was a part of her. The long-missing piece that, once found, made her complete. Her body screamed for release as she worked for it, moving with him in an ever-increasing rhythm. He was so good. So...perfect. These thoughts and more raced through her mind in a blur, tangling her emotions with the sensations dazzling her.

She forced her mind to quiet. Now wasn't the time to worry about what might happen in the still-nebulous future. Wouldn't think about what she was feeling beyond the incredible pleasure erupting inside her. But though she forced her thoughts to stillness, Nicole knew that, sometime soon, she'd have to explore them.

It wouldn't be a one-night fling, but what she had with Griffin was still temporary. There was no future here. There was only the really fabulous present.

"Stay with me," he whispered, taking her mouth in a fierce kiss.

"Right here," she assured him, and slid her

hands up and down his back. She loved the feel of him beneath her palms. So hot, so strong… so *hers*.

Coiled tension strung even tighter at her center. Nicole reached for it, working, straining, moving with him as he set a fast, hard rhythm. Again and again, they separated and came together. Their bodies moved as one, their sighs and gasps sounded out in the moonlit darkness, creating a cocoon of heat and desire that tightened around them until they were both lost in the quest for the release that lay just out of reach.

She looked up into Griffin's eyes and leaped into the passion she read there. Her hands fisted on his broad back, Nicole called out his name and surrendered to the moment, her body quivering, trembling with the force of her climax.

Moments later, Griffin kissed her and with a harsh, gut-wrenching groan, gave himself up to that same overwhelming release.

His body exploded into hers, and when the fire between them died, she held him close to her heart and deliberately let go of tomorrow.

*** * ***

"At least the hammering has stopped."

"For now."

Nicole looked over at Lucas, standing alongside Griffin, and for a second, her mind went blank. Two gorgeous men across the room from her and she was sleeping with one of them.

Well, okay, not *sleeping*.

For the last three days, whenever someone else was around, she and Griffin had pretended to get on each other's nerves. And every night, they'd taken turns simply getting on each other.

How had her life gotten so complicated?

"Want juice, Mommy!"

Oh, thank God, was all she could think as she looked down at Connor. She could always count on her son to ground her in reality. Whatever she and Griffin had was like a slice out of time, an alternate reality where a powerful, gorgeous, rich man spent every night in her bed.

Great place to visit, but she knew she couldn't live there. She didn't have a place in Griffin's life. But for now, it was enough to have a place in his bed.

"Sure, sweetie." Nicole walked to the fridge and opened it. She grabbed Connor's sippy cup, filled it with apple juice and stood up again. That's when she saw Connor in Griffin's arms. Her heart fisted. Her lover and her son. Griffin was tickling Connor's belly and the music of her little boy's laughter filled the room.

"He's a great kid," Lucas said. "Almost three now, right?"

"Yes," she answered, walking over to hand the juice to Connor. "He's growing up so fast."

"Yeah, and he's got a hell of an arm, too," Griffin said, turning his head to avoid Connor's swinging hand.

Lucas's eyebrows went up. "You're playing ball with him?"

"He does?" Nicole asked at the same time.

Griffin looked from one to the other of them, and if she was reading his expression correctly, he almost looked embarrassed for people to find out he was playing with Connor.

"Yeah, I tossed the ball with him a little this morning when I dropped him off at preschool."

"You dropped him—" Lucas started.

"I had an appointment and Griffin helped me out," Nicole said quickly. She didn't want Lucas thinking that she and Griffin were a couple, after all. "He was doing me a favor because he does owe me for burning down my kitchen."

"We agreed that was an accident," Griffin muttered.

Safe ground, was all she could think. One of their arguments that should keep convincing people that they were nothing more than roommates by happenstance.

"Yes," she agreed. "An accident that wouldn't have happened if you hadn't decided I needed help even after I told you I didn't."

"Just because you *can* do something yourself doesn't mean you have to."

"You know," Lucas interrupted.

"And just because you *can* help doesn't mean you should," Nicole said, gaze fixed on Griffin.

"Arguing about it—" Lucas said.

"Accepting help doesn't mean you have to let go of your pride, you know. Pride isn't always the most important thing in the world."

"Says the man with an ego the size of the planet."

"Ego's not pride," Griffin countered.

"And sometimes pride is all some of us have to hold on to," Nicole countered, and plucked Connor from Griffin's arms. With her little boy tucked against her, she stared up into the blue eyes that were now so familiar to her.

She looked into them every night as they made love and found them watching her every morning when she woke up. She knew Griffin's moods now and could practically read what he was thinking in his eyes. And right now, she thought, he was irritated and barely bothering to conceal it.

This little conversation had started out as just another of their ploys to keep people from guessing what was going on between them, but somehow it had taken a turn toward truth. Fine, she wasn't really angry at him anymore for the kitchen fire. But he had yet to admit that it had happened simply because he hadn't believed her capable of doing something on her own. Pride?

That was the one thing about her he *should* understand.

Nicole had known the Kings for more than a year now, and a more prideful bunch didn't exist. She would be willing to bet a fortune she didn't even have that there wasn't *one* of them that would willingly let go of his pride.

Well, she wasn't a King, but her pride was just as important to her as theirs was to them. And it didn't hurt to remind Griffin of that.

Turning to Lucas, she asked, "Did you ever hear from my insurance company?"

He glanced at Griffin, then looked back at her. Responding to the glint in her eye, he straightened up and said, "Yeah. I did. We're good to go with the remodel, except," he added with an uncomfortable wince, "for the deductible."

"I know." Nicole wanted to wince, too. She really hated raiding her already-small savings account to pay for a remodel that hadn't been in her budget at all. But the upside, she reminded herself, was that once the deductible was met and the work done, she'd have a lovely kitchen where everything worked. Best to hold on to that thought.

"I'll take care of the deductible," she said, lifting her chin. "I'll have a check for you tomorrow."

"Nicole—"

"My house, my problem." She faced Griffin and met his gaze squarely, not flinching at all from the banked anger she saw there.

"Fine," he ground out. "You want to be stubborn, go ahead."

"Wow, so gracious of you to *allow* me to pay my bills and meet my responsibilities," Nicole said. "Thanks so much."

"Play ball?" Connor asked.

"Not now, sweetie," Nicole said at the same time that Griffin answered, "Sure."

Lucas rolled his eyes.

Nicole narrowed her gaze on Griffin. "It's Connor's naptime."

"Doesn't look tired."

"My son," she said. "My call."

A long, humming second passed before Griffin scowled and nodded. "Fine."

Still holding Connor tight, Nicole headed out of the room. She paused in the doorway to look back at the men watching her. Lucas looked wary, but Griffin's expression was a mixture of disgust and tightly reined anger. Well, he'd have to get used to the fact that Nicole ran her own life. She didn't need a big, strong man making her decisions or paying her way. She didn't need his help to raise her son, either. She'd gotten along fine on her own before he swept into her life, and she'd do just fine again once he was gone.

Although she didn't like the sound of the word *gone*.

They were playing a strange game. Lovers at night, friendly enemies by day. He'd become a part of her routine, the two of them sharing everything from kitchen duties to time spent with Connor. They were building a relationship on a foundation that didn't exist.

This was the craziest thing she'd ever done, yet she couldn't bring herself to regret it.

Lovers or enemies?

Nicole wasn't sure which was the truth anymore. Or if either was.

* * *

"Okay," Lucas said when she was gone. "That was awkward."

"Yeah." Griffin walked to the fridge, opened it and grabbed two beers. He straightened up and tossed one of them to his cousin. "Welcome to my world."

"She's still completely pissed at you over the kitchen."

"Seems that way," Griffin mused, tossing a glance at the empty doorway. A sizzle of irritation buzzed inside him. Damn woman had a head like a rock. Hell, she should have been born a King. She would have fit right in with the rest of them.

But if she'd been a King, he wouldn't be having her now, and that he couldn't imagine. Still, the game they were playing was getting harder to put up with.

Yeah, most of what had just passed between them had been an act. Keep up the tension between them in front of other people so no one would suspect what was really going on. But,

Griffin thought, what she had said also carried enough truth to be convincing.

Her damn pride was almost as tough as his. Objectively, he could understand that and respect it. But right now it was getting in his way and that was unacceptable.

Like the damn deductible for her insurance payout. He knew she didn't have that kind of money to spend, but would she ask for help? No. She blamed him for the fire, but would refuse to allow him to pay for the blasted deductible. What the hell kind of sense did that make?

Lucas laughed and brought Griffin out of his thoughts.

"Damn, cuz, you're living a rough life here, aren't you?" He shuddered dramatically. "She's riding you every day, isn't she?"

"As often as possible," Griffin muttered, his mind providing images of Nicole rising up over him in the night, holding his body in hers, riding him to an explosive—

"Look," Lucas said agreeably, unknowingly shattering Griffin's thoughts, "I know what life is like when you're living with a woman who's mad at you for some damn thing or other. How about I help you out? We had a job wrap up last night. So I can put an extra crew on Nicole's job, wrap it up faster."

Faster. Get Nicole back into her own home that much sooner. In theory, a good thing. In reality, not. When she was back home, whatever was between them would end. That was their new agreement. If she was back in her familiar world, it would reset their relationship—or whatever the hell it was—and there'd be no more nights with her.

Their summer affair would be over.

His hand fisted around the bottle of beer. Griffin wasn't ready for it to be over. On the heels of that realization came a quick mental disclaimer: it wasn't that he wanted a *permanent* thing with Nicole. Nothing like that. But he *did* want more than a measly few days.

"No," he heard himself say. Lucas looked at him with surprise.

"Seriously? Why the hell not?"

Good question. "Because there's no hurry," he muttered, "that's why not."

"Uh-huh." Lucas took a drink of his beer and leaned against the kitchen counter. "Sell that to somebody else, because I'm not buying it."

Griffin gave his cousin the nearly legendary King freezing stare, designed to shake anyone who dared cross a King. Problem was, it didn't work on the family. Lucas merely shook his head in pity.

"Fine. You don't have to buy it, Lucas."

"Right." He snorted. "You're trying to freeze me out, and it's not working."

"What will?" Griffin asked.

"Nothing," Lucas assured him unnecessarily. "So, the thing is, you're in no hurry to get Nicole out of here, even though she's making you miserable."

Miserable?

Hell, she was making him *nuts.*

He looked away from his cousin and let his gaze slide across Rafe and Katie's sun-washed kitchen. This place had become a second home to him over the past week or more. And memories were crashing over him. Nicole and him here, in this kitchen, having ice cream at midnight and laughing like a couple of kids. Him, plopping a naked Nicole down on the edge of the counter and her legs coming around his waist, pulling him deep into her heat until neither of them could have said where one of them ended and the other began.

Yeah, she was making him crazy.

And he didn't want it to end.

At least not yet.

Frowning at his cousin, Griffin told him, "Don't make anything out of this."

"Oh, it's already been made, and I'm not the one who did it," his cousin said with a smirk. "You think I can't read your face? Poker was never your game, Griff. Garrett's the one with the unreadable expression. Yours is an open book."

Irritation flooded him. He was a damn security expert, for God's sake. He made a living by being hard to read. What the hell was Nicole doing to him? "Well, quit reading it."

"Too late now," Lucas said, hooting with laughter. "Damn, cuz. With Katie's *best friend?*"

Some of the King family brawls were legendary. Once Adam and Travis had a knock-down, drag-out fight that went on for nearly eight hours. It had started at a family picnic, when Travis told Adam he had no skill for horse breeding. A lie of course. Adam had a string of some of the best horses in California—hell, anywhere. But Travis liked to get a dig in, and once Adam cut loose, the two of them battled while the rest of the cousins at the picnic made a damn fortune in bets.

It didn't take much to set off guys with too much pride and too little temper control. Plus, it was just plain fun to get into a good fight once in a while. Usually Griffin and his twin could blow off some steam with a friendly fistfight. But since Garrett was off being a damn prince now, it had been a while since Griffin had had anyone to scuffle with. So if Lucas didn't lay off fast, there was going to be a fight.

"Let it go, Lucas."

"Sure," Lucas said, laughing. He held up both hands. One empty, one still clutching his beer. "That'll happen." He took a hard look at Griffin's expression. "Hey, hey, not looking for a fight. After the last time Rafe and I got into it, Rose told me she'd kick my ass if I came home battered again."

"Hiding behind your wife?"

"Damn straight. She's scarier than you," Lucas said, still laughing, damn his eyes. "You do know that when Katie gets back, if she finds out what you're up to, you're dead meat."

"Yeah," Griffin said, taking a long sip of his beer. "I know."

Katie wouldn't hit him, but he'd never get another cookie in his whole, miserable life. And siding with his wife might cause Rafe to go all fury and fists on him, but Griffin wasn't too worried about that. He could take Rafe.

Still, he didn't like the idea of creating trouble in the family. And Nicole was seriously trouble. But if he had a choice between keeping things in the King family on an even keel or having Nicole, then the choice was a simple one. The family would get over a shakeup. He wasn't ready to let Nicole go yet.

"You're either in really deep," Lucas said with a shake of his head, "or you're nuts. Not sure which."

"Might be both, I'm not thinking about it."

"Not a good sign, cuz."

"Tell me about it," Griffin muttered darkly. He was a man who *always* knew what was next. The man with a plan. Always. He didn't do a damn thing without knowing the consequences and what his response would be. In the security business, you'd better have a backup plan—and a plan for when that one went bottom up, too.

Only one other time in his life had he just gone with his heart instead of thinking things through logically, and that had turned to crap in a microsecond. So what were the chances this thing with Nicole wouldn't go south in a big way someday soon?

Zip.

And wouldn't you just know Lucas would pick up on what was going on? Most of his cousins would have been oblivious, too concerned with what was going on in their own lives to be working out someone else's secrets. Figured he had to be dealing with one who noticed more than the job at hand.

"Seriously, man," Lucas said with a slow shake of his head, "hope it's worth the trouble."

"Me, too," Griffin muttered. The icy cool of the beer bottle in his hand was no match for the heat that streamed through him at the mere thought of Nicole.

So that was his answer. She was worth family trouble. She was worth the fight he and she would be having as soon as Nicole realized he'd already paid her deductible on the fire insurance. And worth the battle they'd have the second she found out he'd authorized upgrades she hadn't approved for her kitchen.

Yeah. She was worth it.

And that worried him.

"Okay, it's your funeral," Lucas told him and pushed away from the counter.

"Thanks for the support."

"Hey, I'm supportive," Lucas argued. "I'm just not an idiot."

"Thanks again."

Lucas grinned and shot a glance at the doorway through which Nicole had disappeared. "So while she's busy with Connor, you want to talk about the upgrades for Nicole's kitchen?"

Nodding, Griffin said, "Let's take our beers next door to talk about it, though. Don't want to chance her overhearing."

"Yeah," Lucas agreed, already heading for the back door. "Me neither. I'm doing these changes on your authorization, not hers. Hell, if she wanted to, she could *sue* King Construction."

"She won't sue you."

"I'm gonna hold you to that."

"Go ahead. Nicole won't sue." She'd be mad as hell, but her fury would be aimed at Griffin, not Lucas. Griffin followed him out the door, then just to be mean, added, "She'll turn your wife on you."

"Oh, man." Lucas looked back at him. "That's cold."

"Women are dangerous people, cousin," Griffin said, looking over his shoulder at the empty room behind him.

"You can say that again, cuz," Lucas was saying, walking toward the gate in the fence and

Nicole's house beyond. "But what would we do without them?"

"That's the question," Griffin murmured.

Too bad he didn't have an answer.

Seven

The following day, Connor was at preschool, and Nicole was back at Sandy's place with a question about that week's billing. Not that she'd had a chance to ask it yet.

"So how's the kitchen coming along?" Sandy asked.

"I'm not sure." Nicole flipped through her friend's business file, looking for one page in particular. "I haven't actually seen it since the first day Lucas had his crew in."

"What?" Sandy peeled the paper off her lemon cupcake and took a bite. As she chewed, she asked, "Are you *nuts?* It's your kitchen. How can you not be curious about what they're doing in there?"

Nicole found the paper she was looking for and slid it across the table to Sandy. "I was there when they were using sledgehammers to take out my grandmother's cupboards and the ceiling. I saw a gigantic hole in the floor and looked straight down at the dirt." She shuddered. "Way more than I wanted to see, so no thanks. I don't want to see any more destruction in there."

"But it's *con*struction now. They're fixing it all up."

"And it'll be great when they're finished. Meanwhile, Griffin's keeping an eye on what they're doing and he tells me it looks terrific."

"A guy?" Sandy shook her head as if she was hearing things. "You're taking a *guy's* word for what your remodel looks like?"

"Griffin's there every day. He's been working with the crew and—" And it was too hard to keep up the pretense of disinterest around others, Nicole thought.

Just yesterday, sniping at Griffin in front of Lucas had started as part of their game, but had gone off on a tangent that had felt all too real. And she didn't want real at the moment. She wanted her fantasy to continue.

When Lucas was gone, she and Griffin hadn't talked at all about the pseudo-argument, but she knew he was still thinking about it, just as she was. She couldn't help it if he thought she was being stubborn. Nicole took care of her own bills. She stood on her own two feet. She wasn't about to start looking around for a man to sweep in and rescue her.

Even if the fire *had* been his fault.

Sandy tapped her fingernails against the tabletop. "This makes no sense to me…unless this isn't about avoiding your kitchen at all."

Nicole glanced at her. "What else would it be?"

"You said Griffin's over there every day. Maybe you're trying to avoid him."

She laughed. "I'm *living* with him, Sandy. Hard to avoid."

"Uh-huh."

"What?"

"Oh, nothing. Just that you haven't touched your double-fudge cupcake. Every time you say the name *Griffin* you look away. *And* you look like a woman who's been having regular sex."

This time her laugh sounded nervous, even to herself. "Excuse me?"

"Oh, come on. I know that wow-am-I-a-lucky-woman look." She winked. "I see it every time I look in the mirror."

"You're way too perceptive."

"It's a gift."

"You should return it," Nicole told her, grabbing up her cupcake for a deliberate bite. Flavor exploded in her mouth and she nearly groaned. Sandy might be irritating, but she was a hell of a good baker.

"Okay," her friend demanded, "so give me details. You never did tell me how the night of magic orgasms went."

"Why should I?"

"Because it was my idea for you to have this fling."

True. If Sandy hadn't suggested it, Nicole might never have made that move out in the hot tub. And then she would have missed…a lot.

"It was a good idea," she admitted with a sigh.

"How good?"

Talking to Katie was out of the question, and if Nicole didn't talk to someone soon, she'd burst. And Sandy was right, it *had* been her idea. Who better to talk things over with?

"So excellent," Nicole heard herself say, "that one night wasn't enough."

Sandy blinked. "The fling continues?"

"It does." Oh, boy did it.

Every time she told herself that was the best it could ever be, Griffin touched her again and set the bar a little higher. The man really did have magic hands. And a magic mouth. And a magic—oh, God, she really was getting herself deeper and deeper into a situation she wasn't going to want to get out of.

She was in trouble. She was starting to feel things for Griffin she had no business feeling, and she didn't have the slightest clue how to turn them off.

"Interesting." Sandy leaned back in her chair, and Nicole stopped searching for the order sheet to meet her friend's steady stare.

"Interesting. Sure. That's one word for it."

Another word might be *dangerous.* Or *sexy.* Or *tempting.*

"And was it your idea to keep the fling flinging, so to speak?"

Nicole laughed shortly. "No, it was his."

"Really?"

"Don't make this more than it is," Nicole warned Sandy, and realized it was the same warning she kept giving herself. She'd known that Sandy would react just like this, but if she could find a way to convince her friend this affair meant nothing, then maybe Nicole might eventually believe it, too. "It's a fling, Sandy. More than a one-night stand, but a fling. That's all."

"A fling would have been flung already," Sandy said thoughtfully. "In one glorious night. Fling and move on. But this isn't, is it?"

"It's not over, but it's like a really long one-night stand, that's all." Good for her. She sounded firm. "No strings. No promises. That's a fling."

"That's an affair. You're having an affair."

Well, that sounded…uncomfortable. And so not like her. An affair? Nicole shifted on the chair and took another bite of her cupcake. An affair implied a relationship. But she and Griffin didn't have a relationship. Did they? Okay, yes, they lived in the same house. They had meals together every day. They laughed and fought and made up. They shared a bed together every night—but, that was just *sex,* right?

Her stomach jittered a little as her thoughts flew in crazy circles around and around in her mind.

Sex was just that. But after sex, they didn't split up and go to separate rooms. They slept in the same bed. Woke up together. Laughed together. Played with Connor together. Heck, they even shared duties around the house—everything from cooking to bathing Connor and doing laundry. That was a relationship, wasn't it? Oh, God, was she sliding into something she hadn't wanted? Hadn't been looking for?

"Uh-oh," Sandy muttered, "you look awfully pale all of a sudden."

"No," Nicole argued, "I'm not. I'm…fine."

She so wasn't fine.

Sandy just looked at her and shook her head. "You're really not, are you?"

"No," Nicole said softly. "I'm not."

Images of Griffin rose up in her mind, like she was flipping through the photo gallery on her phone, except it was a slide show of all Griffin, all the time.

Him this morning, smiling at her over his coffee cup. Him last night, carrying Connor to bed, with the little boy's giggles trailing behind them like a bright ribbon floating on the air. Griffin leaning in to kiss her as he used his body to push hers into heaven. Griffin sitting with Connor on his lap, reading the little boy a story and cuddling both Connor and the stuffed alligator close.

Griffin in the hot tub, holding out a glass of wine to her as she joined him. Making love under the shade of the elm tree in the yard. Griffin, a streak of grease across his forehead, bending over her car to fix the radiator. The picnic they'd had in the living room, candlelight dancing on the walls in softly shaded shadows.

There *was* more between them than she had realized. She didn't know what it was, didn't know how long it would last, but the one thing she was sure of was that when it ended, it was going to hurt. Bad.

She'd walked into this, completely sure of herself and her decision. Nicole had been so certain she could have a little fling without letting her heart get involved. Turned out that she just wasn't the have-an-orgasm-or-two-and-move-on kind of girl.

"Oh, God."

"Sweetie…"

She came up out of her thoughts to see soft concern and worry in Sandy's eyes. That pride she and Griffin had fought over reared its head.

Instantly, Nicole shook her head. "This is exactly why I didn't want anyone knowing what Griffin and I were doing. You're different, of course, since you knew even before anything had happened, but Sandy, if you feel sorry for me now, I might scream. Or cry. And I don't want to do either."

"Yeah," her friend said, "but I don't like knowing you're setting yourself up for pain."

"Not my favorite thing, either," Nicole admitted, already dreading the misery she'd feel when whatever it was she shared with Griffin was over. "No, I went into this with my eyes open, and they're still open."

"That's the problem, isn't it?" Sandy asked.

Sighing, Nicole admitted, "Probably. I can see the end coming, Sandy."

"It doesn't *have* to end."

Nicole laughed shortly. "No sympathy *or* delusions, thanks. Of course it has to end. I've known that all along. It's my own fault if I let myself forget that, even for a second."

Taking a deep breath, Nicole changed the subject, because she really couldn't take much more of Sandy's warm, sympathetic gaze. Pretty soon she'd start feeling sorry for herself and where would that get her? Nowhere.

"So—" She tapped one finger on the sheet of paper she had slid in front of Sandy a few minutes before. "How about instead of my love life, we talk about this order from your supplier for the week's flour and sugar? I couldn't make out the amount at the bottom of the bill. Your handwriting sucks. Haven't we talked about you entering all of your bills on the computer?"

As if understanding that her friend was close to the edge, Sandy picked up the paper and smiled. "But if I did that, I wouldn't need *you,* would I?"

"Good point." The only reason Nicole had a successful business was because her clients unilaterally loathed or were confused by the bookkeeping software available.

While Sandy studied her own handwriting as if it was hieroglyphics, Nicole thought about Griffin. Again. About the end that was coming and about the nights she still had to look forward to.

She was making memories, she told herself. Memories that would both comfort and torment her long after this affair with Griffin was over.

"Are the new cabinets in yet?"

"What?" Griffin looked at Nicole over the dinner table. This was getting so damn comfortable, he could hardly remember sitting in his empty condo with a nuked dinner and the sound of silence hanging over him. Funny, but he really wasn't looking forward to having his nights to himself anymore. Okay, maybe that wasn't funny, but it was a little unnerving.

"The cabinets?" she repeated.

"Oh. The cabinets." He nodded and told himself to pay attention. "Yeah, they're in."

And they were light oak instead of pine, but she hadn't asked him that, had she? He frowned down at his dessert. He wasn't sorry he'd been upgrading Nicole's kitchen, but he could at least admit to himself that he was beginning to regret lying to her about it.

"Oh, good. Then the counter should be going in soon, right?"

"Yeah, in a few days." The granite guy they were working with was still searching for the right stone that would match the description Nicole had given Griffin when she'd described her dream kitchen. "They're putting the floor in tomorrow, though."

Nodding, Nicole leaned over Connor and dropped a few sliced strawberries onto his highchair tray. Instantly, the boy made a lunge for them.

Griffin grinned at the action. The boy had sneaked up on him. He hadn't meant to get involved with Connor; it had just happened. Those wide eyes and happy smiles had sucked him right in and now the boy had carved a place for himself in Griffin's heart.

He was going to miss the little guy, he thought, and scowled even more fiercely at his plate.

"Do you think the linoleum I picked out will go with the green walls?"

"Absolutely," Griffin said, dropping a couple of spoonfuls of whipped cream onto his own bowl of strawberries. The cream-colored flooring Nicole had chosen would have been a good match with the wall paint. But it was linoleum—cheap, but hardly the best choice, and it wouldn't last more than five years. The warm, cream-and-green-flecked tiles Griffin had approved instead would look better. And last longer.

She still wouldn't like it, but the deed would be done and unless she wanted to take a hammer to her new tile floor—which he wouldn't put past her—she'd live with it. More, though she might not admit it, she'd *love* the changes to her kitchen.

Sometimes, Griffin told himself, you just had to do the right thing whether other people agreed with you or not. And damned if he'd let her short-change herself because of her damn pride. He was prepared for the battle that would erupt when all of this came out.

He rubbed the back of his neck and listened to Connor's laughter as he chortled at something only an almost-three-year-old would understand.

"My friend Sandy said I was crazy for not keeping an eye on the remodel, but I told her I trusted you," Nicole was saying, and Griffin looked at her. In the overhead light, her blond hair looked bright as sunlight. Her blue eyes met his, and there was a question in those depths that he had no intention of answering.

The fact that she trusted him was working to his advantage here. And God, even thinking that made him feel like a bastard. But he was in too deep to change course now.

"Thanks," he said, swallowing the knot of guilt in his throat along with a mouthful of strawberries. "I appreciate that."

Outside, darkness crouched at the windows, but inside, the kitchen was warm and…cozy, Griffin thought. As soon as the thought appeared, he had to wonder when the last time he'd been around anything cozy had been. He couldn't come up with a single example. Not since he was a kid, anyway. Back then, with his parents still alive and all of his brothers at home, there had been the same sort of feeling he had now: that sense of belonging to something bigger than yourself. To being a part of something.

Well, *that* thought brought him up short. He didn't belong with Nicole and Connor. This was temporary. A blip in his life. Nothing more. Once it was over, he'd go his way, she'd go hers and they'd never have any of this again.

Funny.

That should have made him feel better.

It didn't.

"How much longer before the kitchen's ready?" Nicole asked.

"Not long," Griffin muttered. It seemed his cousin didn't give a damn about Griffin's plans. Lucas wanted this job wrapped up so he and his wife could go visit their cousin Jefferson in Ireland.

So now there were six guys working every day on Nicole's place and in a matter of days, it would

be complete. Added to that, in another week or
so, Rafe and Katie would be back in Long Beach.
This little interlude, or whatever the hell it was,
was almost over.

"Good," Nicole said. "That's…good."

He looked into her eyes and saw the same
glimmer of mixed emotions that he was feeling.
"Yeah, it is."

"Want a story!" Connor shouted and Griffin
shifted his gaze to him.

Strawberries stained the little boy's face and
clung to the wisps of hair falling across his forehead. Innocence shone in the eyes so much like
his mother's, and Griffin felt that soft slide into
affection pick up speed. This was what he'd
wanted to avoid. Hell, he had plenty of practice
disentangling himself from women. But with a
kid, things got messy.

Walking away from Connor's mother would
be hard, but Griffin would be able to do it with
a clean conscience, because Nicole understood.
How the hell did you make a toddler understand
that you weren't a part of his life anymore? How

did you wean yourself away from playing with the boy? From wanting to protect him?

Big mistake this, he told himself. He should have held back from getting involved in anything more than sex with Nicole. But how could he not care for the boy when he was so much a part of the mother who already had Griffin twisted into knots?

"Looks like you need a bath first, kid," he finally said with a laugh.

"Yes, he does," Nicole agreed, already standing to free her son from the chair.

"I'll do it," Griffin offered before he realized the words were coming from his mouth.

"It's my turn," Nicole reminded him. "You had bath duty last night."

He tried to shrug away the offer as if it was no big deal. "If it'll get me out of doing the dishes…"

"No baf!" Connor cried.

Griffin smiled. He could remember being a dirty little boy and fighting to stay that way. And he remembered his mom, harried and busy, overseeing five boys and cleaning the kitchen. But his father had been there to take over bath time and assist in getting Griffin and his brothers into bed.

Pretty soon, Nicole would be on her own again with no one to turn to for a break. For help. Griffin wouldn't be around. He'd be off somewhere in whatever house he bought, filling his nights with anonymous women and meaningless sex— and Nicole and Connor would go on with their lives without him.

Something hard and cold settled in the pit of his stomach. Felt like he'd swallowed a lump of ice. Well, she wasn't on her own yet, he thought, and heard himself say, "No. No tradeoff. Why don't you go sit down and have a glass of wine? I'll take care of Connor and the dishes."

Tipping her head to one side, Nicole looked at him, a confused smile on her face. "What's the occasion?"

He undid the strap across Connor's lap and lifted him out of the seat. Instantly, the little boy hooked his arms around Griffin's neck. The ice in his gut melted a little at the wordless expression of trust from Connor.

"Not an occasion," Griffin said finally, "just a favor."

Nicole walked toward him. "Is this the kind of favor one friend does for another?"

"Is that what we are?" he asked, disbelief coloring his words. "Friends?"

"What else is there?" she asked.

He didn't know the answer, either. The only thing he was sure of was that she wasn't *just* his friend. She was more than that. How much more, he didn't really want to think about.

"Well, now," Griffin murmured, lifting one hand to cup her cheek, "that's an interesting question, isn't it?"

As he carried Connor out of the room, he felt Nicole's gaze locked on him, and he wished to hell he had an answer to his own damn question.

Connor smashed the sand castle with all the vigor of a rampaging Viking. Chortling with glee, he rained tiny fists down onto the damp sand, and Griffin laughed aloud watching the destruction. He turned his head to see if Nicole was watching and when their gazes locked, even from a distance there was nearly a physical punch that hit him hard. He didn't understand it. Usually he would have moved on well before now. Griffin didn't stay interested in a woman once he'd had her. But Nicole was different.

He kept waiting for whatever it was between them to cool off. It hadn't. If anything, it was heating up. She was in his mind all the damn time. He slept with her every night, listening to the soft sighs of her breath. He woke up with her every morning, his arms wrapped around her as she snuggled in close, allowing him to take in the scent of her peach shampoo with every breath. She was ingrained in him now. She'd become a huge part of his everyday world, and he wasn't sure what to do about it. Hell, he couldn't even think about anything but Nicole.

If he wasn't on vacation already, he'd be damned useless.

Even here, surrounded by the dozens of people still on the beach as the sun began setting, Griffin was hard put to keep a grip on his hormones.

"Do more, Griff!"

Connor's voice dragged Griffin back from the

danger zone in his mind. Looking at the smiling face of the little boy staring up at him with adoration, Griffin felt a completely dissimilar kind of jolt. Nicole was hitting him on a lot of levels, but Connor was arrowing straight into Griffin's heart. A different kind of danger entirely. One just as treacherous.

"Okay, little man," he said and scooped the cold sand together into a haphazard tower. Connor's tiny hands worked with him, patting and slapping at the sand. "Gonna help me, are you?"

"Me do it!"

"Attaboy."

When his phone rang, Griffin was almost surprised. When he was working, the damn thing was ringing all the time. But since his vacation started, he'd practically been living in a vacuum. A very sexy, very confusing vacuum.

Still, he carried the phone because, in his business, he always had to have his phone with him. He never knew when a client or the office would need to reach him. He grabbed the phone from the pocket of his cargo shorts, checked the readout on the screen and grinned. "Hey, Garrett—how's life in the palace?"

"Oh, you know how it is," his twin brother said with a laugh. "Another day wearing a crown."

"Yeah." Griffin laughed, too, and reached out one hand to smooth Connor's hair back from his face. "Must be tough. The villagers marching on the castle with flaming torches yet?"

"Nope," Garrett told him. "But my brother-in-law the prince beat the hell out of me in a horse race yesterday. That count?"

"Close enough." The wind ruffled Griffin's hair and tugged at the edges of the T-shirt he wore. The outgoing tide left a wide stretch of damp sand and the ocean shyly sighed toward shore, then slid back out, leaving a stain of wet that glimmered like silver in the late-afternoon sunlight. A couple of surfers bobbed on their boards, and families were packing up their picnic coolers to head home.

Up on the beach behind him, Nicole sat in a beach chair with a book she hadn't been reading. And here at the edge of the water, a little boy destroyed another sand castle.

"Again!"

Smiling, Griffin held the phone with one hand and used his free hand to pile up the wet sand into another doomed tower.

"Did I just hear a kid?" Garrett asked. "Where are you?"

"Yes, you heard a kid," Griffin said, frowning. "There's a lot of them here. I'm at the beach."

"You hate the beach."

Griffin shook his head, then smiled as Connor patted tiny hands against the sand tower. "I don't hate the beach. I hate the crowds." He glanced up and down the shoreline. The sun was sinking and most of the people were leaving. Soon the beach would be empty but for a few diehard surfers and the handful of teenagers who would sit around a fire, drinking beer and telling lies. The wind was cooler and a few clouds streamed across the darkening sky. Behind him, Nicole was headed toward them, her long, lovely legs moving slowly and, he thought, with a deliberate sensuality.

He took a deep breath and focused on his twin's voice, which was practically shouting in his ear.

"Who's the kid?"

"Nicole Baxter's son, Connor," Griffin said, and the little boy looked up with a grin when he heard his name.

"Are you nuts? Katie's friend?"

"I'm not nuts," Griffin said. "I know what I'm doing."

"Uh-huh, that's why you're breaking your no-kids rule."

His twin always had known him too well, Griffin thought in disgust. So much for his "secret" relationship with Nicole. So far both Lucas and Garrett had guessed at the truth. If any more Kings found out, Griffin could kiss his cookie supply goodbye.

"This is different." Or so he kept telling himself. Getting involved with a woman who had a child was a two-way risk, and he knew that all too well. When the relationship inevitably ended, you lost not only the woman, but the child you'd formed an attachment to. He'd experienced that once, years ago, and that ache had stayed with him for a long time.

"I can't believe this."

"I'm not walking down an aisle or anything, Garrett. For God's sake, you sound hysterical."

"I never get hysterical."

"Then quit shouting at me when you're too far away to punch in the face."

Garrett sighed through the phone. "I hope you know what you're doing."

"Always," Griffin assured his brother, although, as Nicole came closer and closer, he sort of doubted himself.

Garrett snorted, but let it go. In an abrupt change of subject, he said, "Look, I'm calling to tell you I've got a guy here in Cadria who wants to hire us to protect his gem collection. He's loaning it to a museum in L.A. and he doesn't trust their security."

"Hah. Good call."

"That's what I told him," Garrett said. "Anyway, I've faxed the information to Janice at your office. You've got to come up with the plan and the details on fees, since you're the one on-site."

Griffin scrubbed one hand across his face and nodded at Nicole as she dropped to the sand beside her son. Now that Connor was in safe hands,

Griffin stood up and walked a few steps toward the water's edge.

Just a few days ago, he'd been wishing for work, something to keep his mind busy. Now he glanced back at the woman and child kneeling in the sand. The sun was setting and the pale wash of golden light lay across the two of them as if they were highlighted in a painting.

Frowning to himself, he turned back to look at the sea and the shimmer of light dancing on the surface of the water.

"Griff?" Garret asked. "You there?"

"Yeah, I'm here. When's he need the estimate?"

"Couple of days. When you've got it, fax it back to me at the palace and I'll take it to him and sell the rest of the deal."

Chuckling, Griffin shook his head. "At the palace," he repeated. "Doesn't that ever seem weird to you? That you live in a castle?"

"All the time, man. All the time," Garrett mused. "But Alex lives here, and I live with Alex."

"Yeah," Griffin said. "I get that."

"Do you?" Garrett laughed a little. "Well, now,

there's a surprise. Aren't you the one who suggested that Alex give up the whole princess thing and move back to California with me?"

Yeah, he had. Griffin hadn't understood why Garrett had been so willing to give up his own life in favor of living in Cadria full-time. Turning your world upside down for a woman just hadn't computed with Griffin.

Now, he got it. Though he didn't really want to consider just *how* he'd come to the realization. Another glance at Nicole and he was rewarded with her smile. His chest tightened, so he looked away quickly.

"I'll go to the office, pick up the papers," Griffin said. "Then I'll get it back to you ASAP."

"Okay..." Garrett said slowly. "Griff, is there something you want to talk about?"

"What is this, a chick flick?" Griffin countered, shaking his head as if his twin could see him. "No, I don't want to talk. There's nothing to talk *about.*"

"Right. How about the situation with Nicole and her *kid.*" Garrett paused and said, "Let's remember the last time you got involved with a single mom."

"Let's not." Griffin's scowl was fierce, but since he was facing the sea, no one could see it.

"It about killed you to lose that boy. He even ran away from his mom and went to you."

"I remember." He didn't want to, but he did. Jamie had been six, and Griffin had been his T-ball coach. He'd relived his own childhood through Jamie, and in a few weeks, he'd come to feel like the boy's father. But when Jamie's mom walked away, he'd lost his relationship with Jamie, as well.

Griffin still remembered the afternoon a crying little boy had shown up at his office. Jamie had run to Griffin, hoping to bring him back into his world. There had been nothing he could do to stop the boy's heartbreak...or his own. He'd returned Jamie to his mother and driven away, vowing never again to get involved with a woman who had a child.

He'd kept that vow. Until now.

"This is different," Griffin insisted, and wasn't sure whom he was trying to convince—himself or Garrett. Lowering his voice, he said, "I feel sorry for the kid. He doesn't have a dad, okay? This thing with Nicole and me isn't permanent, so neither is the situation with Connor. I'm not getting sucked in again. I won't let that happen, so relax."

"Right. If you say so."

"Look, I gotta go." Garrett was way too shrewd. Too able to pick up on nuances that Griffin would prefer be ignored. Maybe it was because Garrett was married now, more used to listening, paying attention. But whatever the reason, Griffin wasn't in any mood to dodge more questions. "I'll get back to you in a day or two."

"Fine. Talk to you then."

He hung up, but didn't turn around. Instead, he stared out at the horizon. Coral, scarlet and gold splashed across the sky and spread brilliant reflections of color on the water. The tide was shifting, heading in closer now, and drenched his bare feet as he stood on the sand.

End of the day.

Which meant the beginning of the night with Nicole.

Yeah, he could understand how a woman could turn a man's world upside down.

Didn't mean he liked it.

Eight

"You don't understand how this works," Griffin said later that night, and Nicole heard the oh, so patient, genius-to-moron tone in his voice.

"Wow, you're right," Nicole said, widening her eyes and blinking a couple of times for the dumb-blonde effect. "I've never had to pay bills or work out a budget. Is it a lot of math?"

A second or two ticked past before Griffin huffed out a breath. "Funny. Very funny. Okay, point made. You're an accountant. You get math."

She got a lot more than that, Nicole thought. Griffin might have thought he couldn't be over-heard when he was talking to his brother at the beach. But she *had* heard him when he told Garrett that he felt *sorry* for Connor. That he and Nicole weren't permanent and so neither was his involvement with her son. Fine. She could accept temporary. She'd known that going in. But where did he come off feeling *sorry* for Connor? Her son wasn't a charity case, starving for male attention.

Well, maybe that wasn't completely right, either. Rafe and Katie spent time with them, and Connor loved Rafe a lot. But under Griffin's attentions the last couple of weeks, Connor had blossomed and Nicole couldn't deny it. She tried so hard to be everything her little boy needed— and still, she could see that having a man in his life made a huge difference.

Damn it.

Irritated, she snapped, "Yes, I understand math, but if it makes you feel better, only the little numbers."

He slapped one hand to his chest and gave her a half bow. "Apologies. Now, you going to keep making me pay, or are you going to help me out with this?"

She swallowed the lingering anger over what she'd heard at the beach. He didn't know that she'd heard him and unless she was willing to open up that particular can of worms right now, which she wasn't, she had to let this go. For now, anyway.

"Depends," she said. "Are you going to keep talking to me in the voice you use to read stories to Connor?"

"Another point. Okay, then," Griffin said, sitting down beside her at the kitchen table. "I didn't mean to offend you."

"Good to hear," Nicole told him, and looked into the blue eyes that had come to mean way too much to her.

She was an idiot. Even knowing this was temporary hadn't been enough to make her guard her heart. Instead, she'd practically *run* into a relationship that was going to end up crushing her.

But for now, working with him might be a sort of bridge from the personal to the impersonal. Because God knew, she needed one.

The overhead light was on, spilling down over the papers spread out over the oak table. Connor was sleeping, and the house was quiet. Usually about now, she and Griffin would be doing something a lot more fun than working. But seeing him poring over numbers and logistics had intrigued Nicole enough to offer her help. Which of course he'd dismissed, and that had only made Nicole more determined to prove to him that she was more than he thought she was.

"So," she said, smiling at him, "you need to come up with an estimate for the security at a museum showing of some historical gems?"

His mouth quirked. "Yeah, that sums it up."

"Okay." She shifted her gaze to the papers in front of her and quickly thumbed through them. "Garrett sent the specs of every important gem in the collection and his suggestions for the security."

"Yeah, Garrett's always got plenty of suggestions." Griffin leaned back in his chair. "He's usually the one putting these things together. I'm the on-the-ground guy, making sure it all holds together, that our men are where they're supposed to be." Sitting up straight again, he leaned forward and braced his forearms on the table top.

"I think he did this on purpose. He knows I hate this kind of stuff."

"I love it," Nicole said. "There's clarity in numbers. They don't lie. They don't change. You can count on them being exactly what they're supposed to be."

"Yeah. Annoying."

She laughed a little and picked up the top sheet. "See, Garrett's wrong about this."

"Garrett? Wrong?" Grinning, he leaned in closer. "You've got my attention. What do you see?"

Here was her chance. To show him what she could do. "Do you and your brother compete on everything?"

"Absolutely."

"All righty then," she said, shaking her head. "Well, you're going to love this."

"Show me."

She used a pen to point at a single line in Garrett's notes. "Garrett's suggested using four men around the sapphire collection."

"Yeah, so?"

"The sapphires, while gorgeous, let me just say, aren't exactly the centerpiece of the collection."

He frowned, but he was watching her with a calculated gaze, as if seeing her in a whole new light. "What is, then?"

"There's a brooch. A really old, really ugly brooch." Nicole fought down the nerves jumping inside her and kept her voice cool as she tapped her finger on the grainy photo. The brooch was a swirl of small stones, set into a starburst pattern that then wrapped around a central piece made to look like a clutch of lilies. "It's not pretty at all, but it *was* a gift from Marie Antoinette to the ancestor of the guy who's loaning them to the museum."

He looked like he wanted to argue and then he said, "But the sapphires are—"

"Gorgeous, and yes," Nicole interrupted before he could speak up, "easily sold off on the black market. But Marie's brooch would make most private collectors sit up and beg for a chance to own it."

"Good point," Griffin said. "I would have seen that eventually, of course…"

"Oh, of course."

"I'm gonna ride Garrett, though, because he didn't notice what you did. So, you see anything else?"

Pleased at the gleam of approval in his eyes, Nicole grabbed another sheet of paper and started to make a list. "The rubies should be shown near the sapphires, of course, because the color compositions will complement each other."

"Naturally."

"Two men on each display," she continued, making notations as her ideas began to fly. "With four stationed around Marie's brooch. Then you've got the diamond room." She paused to sigh over the pictures that didn't do the stones justice. "Tiaras, bracelets, a necklace with more than thirty-five carats of diamonds hanging by slender threads of gold…" She stopped and put a hand to her chest. "Excuse me, I'm having a personal moment here."

He laughed. "I never would have guessed that you loved jewelry." He picked up her left hand. "You don't wear any, except for those tiny gold hoops at your ears."

She pulled her hand free, embarrassed to be caught drooling over faxed images of priceless jewels. The only jewelry she'd ever worn had been her wedding ring. That thought brought up memories of the man who'd walked away without a glance backward. The man who'd been a player—as Griffin was—she reminded herself.

"I don't exactly go places where jewelry is necessary. Doesn't mean I can't admire them."

"You should be draped in diamonds," he whispered, his eyes suddenly smoky and filled with a heat she recognized.

"I don't want diamonds," she whispered. But oh, God, she'd love to have the man who was right now staring at her as if he could eat her up.

"Maybe that's why I want to give them to you."

Not permanent, her mind echoed, replaying a couple of the words that she'd overheard Griffin say to his twin. It was enough to stiffen her spine, thank God. "Contrary to the end, huh?"

He gave her that half smile. "Part of my charm."

"Is that what that is?" she asked.

"Admit it, I've got you right where I want you."

Oh, he really did, she thought, wondering just

how she'd come to this place. She'd gone into it for the fun, but now, that fun had become something else. He already had one foot out the metaphorical door and she— Nicole froze as realization crashed down on her. Oh, God. She was falling in love.

Something she'd planned to *never* do again.

Her heartbeat thundered so fiercely in her chest, she was surprised that Griffin couldn't hear it. There was a knot in her throat threatening to cut off her air. Her mind was churning and not coming up with any idea at all to help her find her way out of this. Worst part? This whole situation had been *her* idea. And now she was caught in her own trap.

"Hey," Griffin said, laying one hand on her arm. "You okay? You went sort of white."

"I'm fine." Liar, liar. She really wasn't anywhere close to fine. She was as far from fine as she could possibly get. "I'm just…I don't know."

"It's probably dealing with all those numbers," he teased. "Always does it to me."

She forced a smile she didn't feel. Her insides were twisted up and tangled. Her heart ached as if something was squeezing it. And she knew, deep in her bones, that this pain was just the beginning.

There was much more coming. Soon.

But she wouldn't let him know. Wouldn't let him see that she had been stupid enough to fall in love with a man who was no doubt already preparing his "See you later, take care" speech. So Nicole took a deep breath and told herself firmly to hold it together. Focus on the math, she thought. Just concentrate on the task at hand and get through this moment and into the next. That was all she could do at this point.

"Funny," she said, "numbers do the opposite for me. Let's just finish the job, okay?"

He frowned a little, his blue eyes narrowing on her face. "Okay. I'm not crazy enough to turn down help when it's offered. But—"

She cut him off. If he was nice to her, she might break. If he was tender or sweet or romantic right now, it would do her in. She might blurt out that her feelings for him had changed. That she didn't feel temporary. That she wanted…more. Might actually make the *huge* mistake of saying the *L* word, and where would that lead? To disaster. Pure and simple.

She knew how he felt already. She'd heard him talking to Garrett, hadn't she? She wasn't permanent. He felt *sorry* for Connor.

Oh, God. Connor. Losing Griffin was going to be so confusing for him. He wouldn't understand that Griffin had only been in his life temporarily. That he'd been the object of pity. Her heart hurt for Connor, and she wondered if she shouldn't just pull back from Griffin now. Do what she could to make this easier on her son, if not on her. But would hurrying his hurt make it easier to understand? And how could she leave now anyway? Her house was still not ready, and she couldn't afford to go anywhere else.

She was going to have to try to protect Connor the best she could while, at the same time, dying a little inside.

Shaking her head, Nicole concentrated on the papers in front of her and completely ignored Griffin's attempt at trying to soothe her. "Okay, then, first, we figure out how many men you'll need to work the job."

"We also have to factor in the laser alarm system, the cameras and computer equipment," Griffin was saying, his voice crisp and cool, businesslike, as if he'd accepted that she wasn't interested in anything more at the moment. "We'll cooperate with the museum's standing security, but I'll want King equipment to bolster it."

She looked up at him and thought again that this had become more than just an affair. This was the first time she'd ever talked numbers with a man without watching his eyes glaze over. A part of her warmed to the idea that they were working together. If things were different, they could have had a future where he came to her for help with his business. They could have, over time, developed trust and cooperation and maybe even—

His cell phone rang. Griffin glanced at the readout, and almost instantly his open features closed up tight. His eyes shut her out and he stood up as he answered.

"Brittany, hi."

Brittany. Griffin's voice dropped to the husky, intimate tone she knew so well and Nicole cringed a little. Oh, dear God, was she *interchangeable* with the other women in his life? Did he use that sexy voice on all of them? And did every woman finally imagine herself in love with him?

Probably, she acknowledged, and didn't know whether that made her feel better or worse.

"It's good to hear from you," Griffin was saying as he walked a few steps across the kitchen. "Yeah, I meant to call you, but well, work's been busy."

Huh. He was on *vacation.* She guessed that was his standard line, used to put off women who got too clingy. So if she called him a few weeks from now, it would be her getting the brush-off, not poor Brittany. God, this was so embarrassing.

"Actually," Griffin said, "I'm with my accountant right now, so it's not a good time to…"

His accountant? Whatever else he said was lost on Nicole. That's what she was. Some nameless grunt helping him out with a little math. If she could have, she would have found the nearest hole and crawled into it.

All of her lovely little fantasies popped like soap bubbles in her mind. Pain opened up inside her and Nicole had to force a sudden film of tears from her eyes. Here it was, she told herself. Proof that she'd made the second biggest mistake of her life.

She'd fallen for a man too much like her ex. Oh, Griffin was a better man than Connor's father, but at the heart of it, he was no different. He wasn't interested in commitment, and if she was dumb enough to let him know that she cared about him, she'd see pity in his eyes. That was one thing she never wanted to go through.

So she'd keep her feelings to herself. She'd go along with their affair until it was over and then she'd curl up with a gallon of ice cream and a couple bottles of wine. Until then…

"Sorry about that," Griffin said, sitting down beside her. "Brittany's an old friend and—"

"You don't owe me an explanation, Griffin. I'm just the accountant." She winced as she said it and would have slapped her own hand across her mouth if it would have called the words back. But she so didn't want to hear him try to explain away one of his old girlfriends.

"Hey," he said, catching her chin and turning her face toward him. "I didn't mean—"

She pulled free, though it cost her, because she loved the feel of his hands on her. But best to get used to doing without, wasn't it? "Doesn't matter. Really. Let's just finish up this proposal."

"Right." He watched her carefully, then said, "The proposal."

Nicole shifted her gaze to the list in front of her and pushed her thoughts into linear compliance. Focus on the math, she told herself. Forget about fantasy. Forget about *what if*s. Take what you have and make the most of it before it's gone.

The hardest thing to admit?

She was pretty sure it was already gone.

The next afternoon, the kitchen phone rang, and Nicole picked it up on the run. Connor was in the backyard and she didn't want to leave him alone for long.

"Hello?"

There was a long pause and then a familiar voice asked, "Nicole?"

She grinned. "Katie, hi. How's the vacation going?"

"Amazing," her best friend said, and Nicole heard the smile in her voice. "Seriously, I love Europe. We stopped in Ireland to see Jefferson and Maura and the kids, then spent a few days in Edinburgh to visit Damian and see his new club."

"Oh, you told me it has a ghost theme. Was it great?"

"Very. And a little scary," Katie admitted. "I think it's actually *haunted*."

A twinge of envy filled Nicole at the wonderful things her friend was seeing, experiencing. One day, she promised herself, she, too, would see the world.

"Okay, that actually sounds like fun."

Katie laughed. "You're braver than me, then. Anyway, after we left Damian's we spent a few days in London and, oh, my God, Nicole, it's just…"

Nicole sighed. "I can hear it in your voice."

Still laughing, her friend said, "Good, because I don't think I can describe it. Anyway, after that, we went to Switzerland and now we're in Italy and I think I'm in love with this place. The food alone is orgasmic."

"I'm so jealous," Nicole said.

"I'm jealous of *you*." Katie sighed. "You're in Long Beach. As great as this trip's been, I'm so ready to come home. Is that weird?"

"No," Nicole said, moving to the window so she could keep an eye on Connor while she talked. She so understood Katie's feelings.

This interlude with Griffin had been wonderful. Actually too wonderful, she admitted silently. As Katie said, it had been orgasmic. Yet as much as she hated it, she knew that going home would be best. Leaving Griffin and this idyllic time behind her. Get back to normal—though normal would be different now, too. Because after this time with Griffin, her house would feel emptier than it had. Lonelier than it had.

She sighed a little, and Katie must have heard it.

"Nicole," she asked, "is something wrong?"

"No," she answered quickly. Too quickly, it seemed.

"Okay, I don't believe you."

"Why not?"

"For one thing, you're at my house instead of yours. What happened?" Katie's voice dropped into a serious tone that brooked no argument. "Did Griffin do something? Do I have to kill him?"

So much for secrets. Nicole glanced out the window at Connor, digging happily in the flowerbeds. No matter what else happened in her life, Nicole thought, she had her son. That would get her through anything.

"No," she said finally, "you don't have to kill Griffin."

"Oh, God," Katie groaned. "You slept with him, didn't you?"

Shaking her head, Nicole took the phone from her ear and stared at it in wonder. It was like her friend had X-ray vision or something. "How can you tell that through the phone?"

"Easy. I know the King men." Clearly disgusted, Katie muttered, "I told him to stay away from you. Heck, I told *all* of them to stay away from you."

"Yeah, so Griffin told me. Thanks for that, by the way. What am I, twelve?"

"No," Katie said quickly, "but you're vulnerable and they're all so..."

"Oh, they really are."

"Damn it."

"It's not his fault anyway, Katie. Griffin was staying away," Nicole told her with a sigh. "I went after him."

"Oh." Katie was quiet for a minute. Then, "I don't know what to say, I guess. But, Nicole..."

"Look, something happened at my house and I couldn't stay there and—"

"What happened?"

"Griffin accidentally started a fire in my kitchen and I didn't have a place to stay, so Griffin offered to let us move in here while Lucas and his crew fixed my kitchen and..." She was talking too fast and couldn't seem to stop herself.

"A *fire*?"

"A small one."

"Oh," she said with a laugh, "well, then."

Nicole blew out a breath. "The point is, my house is almost fixed and I'll be moving home soon…" Did she sound as depressed about that as she felt?

"And what about you and Griffin?" Katie asked. "You're telling me you can just walk away without a second thought?"

"I am," she said, and wished she meant it.

"Sweetie, that's just not who you are. But sorry to say, it *is* who Griffin is. Nicole, you have to know what he's like. He's commitment-phobic. Seriously. I mean, Rafe was a challenge, but Griffin is impossible. Being single is like a religion to him."

"Yeah, I know," Nicole told her, leaning on the kitchen counter. With her free hand, she brushed at a few toast crumbs she had missed after Connor's lunch. "Katie, I'm not looking for a husband, remember? And if I was, I wouldn't be looking at Griffin."

My God, could your tongue actually fall off from an overload of lies?

"Oh, honey," Katie said on a half groan. "You're in love with him, aren't you?"

Irritation spiked. "How did you get that out of what I said?"

"I notice you're not denying it."

She should. She really should. Otherwise, here came the sympathy train, which she wanted to avoid. But Katie was her best friend, and Nicole couldn't lie to her over the long haul. And let's face it, once Katie got home and found Nicole miserable, she'd know the truth anyway, so what was the point? "Okay, I might be. Maybe. Probably."

"Nicole…"

"Fine. Yes. I am," she said, grinding out each word. "What're you, a master interrogator?"

Katie laughed a little. "I don't even know what to say to you."

"No sympathy, okay?" Nicole interrupted before her friend could get going. "I don't need you to feel sorry for me, really. I'm a big girl. I knew what I was doing, and I'll be fine. Honestly." She lifted her chin and squared her shoulders. "I was doing great on my own before and I will again."

"Of course you will."

"Thank you," she said, glad to have her friend's support.

"But I'm still going to have Rafe beat him up."

Nicole laughed and shook her head as if Katie could see her. "No, you're not. You're not going to tell Rafe. You're going to pretend you don't know any of this."

"Uh-huh. Why would I do that?"

"Because I'm asking you to," Nicole told her.

"I don't know, Nicole. I feel like I should tell Rafe what happened."

She didn't want one more person to know if she could help it. "Just let it go, okay, Katie? This is between me and Griffin, and it's almost over, anyway."

"Damn it," Katie muttered, "Griffin's never getting another cookie from me as long as he lives."

Outside, Connor stood up and headed for the gate between the yards. Nicole leaned toward the window and tilted her head so she could make sure that the, gate was closed. It wasn't. Griffin must have left it open when he went next door.

Connor was going to run right into a construction area.

"I gotta go, Katie. Connor's running off to our house, and the guys are working there."

"Go, go! I'll see you in a few days!"

Nicole hung up and sprinted for the doorway. She was across the yard and through the gate a couple seconds later. Connor was just toddling toward the house and the sound of the construction crew when Nicole came up behind him and swept him off his feet.

He giggled and shrieked when she lifted him into the air before plopping him onto her hip. Here was her world. Safe and secure and held close to her heart. Whatever else happened, she and Connor would get through it all. Together.

"Escape artist, huh?" She grinned and tickled him until he squirmed in delight. "No visiting our house without me!"

Laughing and pointing, Connor looked at the house and said, "Home!"

She followed his gaze. Home. Where they belonged. The two of them. The way it was supposed to be. Maybe it was time to start moving toward the future. Start letting go of the fantasy and take the first step back to normalcy. Nicole started for the house before she could think about it. It was past time to see what was going on in there. Past time to remember who she was and where she really belonged.

Besides, she could at least warn Griffin that Katie knew what was happening between them—and that his cookie connection had been cut off.

She took the back steps quickly, opened the screen door and stepped into a strange new world.

Griffin and Lucas were arguing over something at the counter, their backs to her, so they didn't see her come in. Nicole took a moment to simply stare at what had been done to her grandmother's old, familiar kitchen.

Shaking her head, she looked from the pale-green walls to the light-wood cupboards, from the tiled floor to the *granite* countertop that was exactly the stone she had once described to Griffin. There was a six-burner gas stove on one wall and a brand-new French-door fridge on another.

This wasn't the kitchen she had asked for.

This was her dream kitchen.

The one she couldn't afford.

"Griff!" Connor shrieked and both men spun around to stare at her with matching expressions of guilt.

But it was Griffin's gaze Nicole caught with her own. Then she managed to croak out, "What the hell have you done?"

Nine

"Busted," Lucas muttered.

"I can't believe this," Nicole said, setting Connor on his feet and glaring at Griffin.

"How did you—*why* did you—" She spun in a tight circle, sending her hair into a blond wave around her head before she stopped abruptly and glared at him again. "You had no right."

Griffin gritted his teeth and faced the fury of the woman across from him. He'd known this moment would arrive, he just hadn't expected it this soon. Lucas and the crew still had some finishing work to do, so Griffin had thought he would have a couple of days before this particular fight. Now that it was here, though, there was no avoiding it.

"Nicole, this is your dream kitchen."

"Yeah, it is," she said. "And one day I would have had it."

"Instead, you have it now," he said, refusing to acknowledge the cold, clipped tone to her voice. "What's the difference?"

"Are you crazy?" she countered. "The difference is that I would have paid for it. I can't afford this now."

"It's all been paid for," Lucas offered, and she turned her glare on him.

Jabbing a finger toward Griffin, she asked, "Yes, paid for by whom? *Him?* How is that ethical? What kind of business are you running anyway, Lucas?"

"Ethical?" He stiffened and shot a quick look at Griffin. "I'm damn ethical, and we did some great work here."

"Work that I didn't order," she reminded him. "I didn't sign off on any of this." She gulped in a breath. "I could sue you!"

Lucas shot a hard look at Griffin.

"Relax," he said, "she's not going to sue King Construction."

"Really?" Nicole argued. She folded her arms over her chest and tapped the toe of one foot against the gleaming tiles in a furious rhythm. "Know me that well, do you?"

"Yeah, Nicole," Griffin said, taking his life in his hands to move a step closer to her. "I think I do. You're pissed right now, but once you've had time to think it over, you'll realize I was right to do this."

"Oh, that's so not going to happen," she muttered darkly.

"If it helps," Lucas put in, "Griff meant it as a surprise for you. He's covered all the bills insurance won't cover."

"Not helping," Griffin said without looking at his cousin.

"Has he?" Nicole's gaze narrowed on Lucas briefly, but it was long enough to have the man taking one long step to the side of Griffin. Obviously, he was trying to stay out of range.

"A surprise." Nicole glanced down at Connor to make sure her son was nearby, then she lifted her gaze to Griffin again. "Flowers are a surprise. A box of chocolates. A damn teddy bear. Not a *kitchen!*"

"Gotta admit, you *were* surprised," he said and shrugged as if completely unaffected by her fury.

"And you thought I'd like this."

"Of course you like it," Griffin ground out. "Hell, you *love* it. You're just too stubborn to admit that you're glad I took care of the changes."

She just blinked at him and a corner of Griffin's mind warned him that that wasn't a good sign.

"You are unbelievable." Her breath huffed in and out of her lungs. "What made you ever think even for a second that I would want you to do this? I *told* you I didn't need your help."

And he was tired of hearing it. What was he, blind? "Yes, you told me that. But it's bull. You *do* need my help, you just don't want it." Griffin crossed his arms over his own chest, deliberately mimicking her stance. "Well, too damn bad, Nicole. You got it whether you want it or not."

"The last time that happened, there was a *fire.*"

He winced, but stood his ground.

She looked at Lucas. "Rip it out. All of it."

Lucas actually paled.

Griffin's temper snapped. "Now who's being crazy? He's not going to destroy a kitchen he just finished building. Take a look around, Nicole. This is the room you described to me. The tiles. The color of the paint. The damn granite that the guy spent two weeks looking for!"

She only stared at him. "I didn't ask you for this, Griffin. What I told you was a dream. Idle imagination."

"And now it's not."

This wasn't going at all the way he'd hoped it would. He knew she'd be pissed, of course, but he'd thought that seeing the kitchen of her dreams right there in front of her would take the sting out. And okay, yeah, he'd expected her to thank him for going to all the trouble of making sure she got what she damn well deserved.

"It wasn't up to you to do this, Griffin," she said, and her voice was softer, lower, as if most of the anger had drained away. But her eyes belied that supposition. They were still flashing, still furious.

"Look, it's done." And even he wasn't sure

why it had been so important to him to give her this. He only knew it had been, and now that it was done, he wanted her to enjoy it. To cook in it every day. To remember him every time she walked into the room.

Griffin frowned as that thought flashed in his mind. Where had that come from? Shifting uncomfortably, he ignored the truth he'd just stumbled on and asked, "Why don't you at least take the time to look around?"

"Yeah, uh," Lucas said, gathering his clipboard from the shining granite countertop. "I'll be going. You two work this out, and let me know who wins."

Nicole shot him a look that should have curled his hair. But clearly Lucas was accustomed to dealing with furious women. He just gave her a smile and slipped out of the room like a damn ghost. So much for family loyalty, Griffin told himself. Who knew a King could be a coward?

Well, fine. He could handle Nicole on his own. He'd been doing it for almost three weeks, right? He knew her, body, heart and mind, and he knew damn well that underneath all of her protests, she wanted this kitchen.

"Go ahead, Nicole. Look." Even God was on his side in this, Griffin thought, since the late-afternoon sunlight washed across the dream kitchen in a sweep of gold. The pale-oak cabinets looked as golden as the light. The floor gleamed, and the granite countertop shone like a mirror.

He ran one hand over the granite and her eyes were drawn to the motion. "It's exactly as you described it," he said softly.

She swallowed hard and scooped up Connor when he would have scuttled out of the room. "I know. And it's even more beautiful than I imagined it would be."

"And the stove." He moved toward the professional-grade appliance. "Six burners, and they all work."

A smile teased at the corners of her mouth, but disappeared way too fast. "It doesn't change anything, Griffin—"

"The fridge I had to guess at, since you didn't really say one way or the other." He pulled open the doors and let her stare into the interior. Boxes of Connor's favorite juice drinks were on the top shelf, and in a wine rack was a bottle of champagne he'd planned to spring on her later.

He watched her expression, and in spite of the anger still churning inside her, he could see how much she loved her new kitchen. Her gaze swept over the tile floors and across the freshly painted walls and landed, for just a minute, on the rooster teakettle he had cleaned up. An unexpected emotion rushed through him and caught Griffin by surprise.

This had started out as a way to pay her back for what he'd done to her house. Then it had become a way to please her, more for his own sake than anything else, he could silently admit. He had wanted the fun of giving her something she hadn't expected. But now it was more than all of that. He wanted her to have it because he knew how important it was to her. The dream she'd described had been too detailed to be just idle wishful thinking. Watching her eyes as she'd told him had convinced him that this dream meant more to her than even she had known.

And besides all of that, he realized now, he'd

wanted her to have it so that she'd never forget him. So that his presence would be stamped on her house. Her world. He wanted her to remember him long after he was gone, because Griffin knew he wouldn't be forgetting her.

"It's really beautiful, Griffin," she said on a sigh. "But that's not the point."

"Then what is the damn point, Nicole?" Annoyance chewed on him. He kept his voice low and even because he didn't want to scare Connor, who was watching him through wide blue eyes. "Tell me, because from where I'm standing, I did something nice for you and I'm getting slapped by it."

Shaking her head, she looked around the kitchen again, and when she finally turned her gaze back to Griffin, she said, "Don't you get it? You doing all of this—" she waved one hand in the air, as if to encompass the entire room "—it's like you're *paying* me to have sex with you."

"What?" Okay, that he hadn't expected. Insult slammed home, and he gaped at her in astonishment.

"It's the big payoff," she continued. "Most men

give tennis bracelets or a necklace or something—"

As she spoke, guilt and something he thought
might be *shame* nibbled at him. That's exactly
what he did when he walked away from which-
ever woman he was spending time with. Usually
he didn't even bother buying the trinket himself. He simply had his assistant, Janice, pick up
something at the jewelry store and send it in his
name. Did those women feel like Nicole did? He
wondered but had no answer.

But that wasn't important here, was it?

"That's insane. And insulting," he added, before grinding his teeth again. "I don't pay for
sex."

"Ah, well," Nicole said, "You don't have to, do
you? Women just line up and take their turns,
hoping you'll smile down on them, is that it?"

Uncomfortable with the shift in conversation,
he tried to turn it back. "Where the hell is this
coming from?"

"I'm sorry, am I not being grateful enough?"
she asked, bouncing Connor on her hip. The lit-

tle boy didn't look happy, and Griffin knew just
how the kid felt.

Before he could think about it, he snatched
Connor from Nicole and held the boy up close
against his chest. Connor leaned his head
on Griffin's shoulder and sighed. "Griff play
ball?"

"Soon, buddy," he promised and ran one hand
down the boy's back in a comforting pat.

"Griff, wanna play." The little boy gave his best
begging smile and a curl of something warm settled in Griffin's chest.

"Pretty soon, kiddo," he said, then turned to
look back at Nicole. "Now how about we just
get down to it? I wanted to do something nice
for you," he started.

"I didn't want you to—"

"Contrary to popular belief, I don't need your
permission to do a damn thing."

"To my kitchen you do."

"Apparently not," he mused and leaned back
against the cold granite counter. New tack, he
thought. Don't fight fury with fury. Instead,

brush it off. Let her know that her anger wasn't changing anything.

"Your cousin—"

"Is out of this. I told Lucas to do it, so your issue is with me, not him."

"Oh," she said with a grimace, "trust me, I know who I have issues with."

"Good, then let's get this settled now." He moved in closer and she didn't budge an inch. "I set fire to the kitchen. It's my job to see it fixed."

"The way I can afford it."

"Fixed. Why the hell are you fighting me on this?"

"Because I take care of myself, Griffin."

"Who's arguing?" he demanded and jiggled Connor when the boy made a sound of distress. "You're the most self-sufficient person I've ever known. I respect that. Hell, you're smart and funny and capable and—"

"Your accountant?"

He stopped, took a breath and blew it out again. That phone call from Brittany kept biting him in the ass. He hadn't meant to insult Nicole; he just hadn't wanted to talk to Brittany any longer than he absolutely had to. And now that he thought about it, he'd given Brittany a diamond necklace. Damn.

"You're more than that to me," he finally said.

"Really, what am I then?"

There was that question again, he thought wildly. And he still didn't have a complete answer. All he knew was, Nicole had touched him on levels he hadn't even been aware of having before her. Levels he wasn't entirely comfortable acknowledging even to himself.

He couldn't give her an answer, so instead, he asked, "Is it so hard to accept that this was important to me?"

Confusion gleamed in her eyes, but at least, he thought, the raw anger was gone.

"Yes," she said softly, "I guess it is. Why, Griffin? Why was this important to you?"

He shoved one hand through his hair, looked down at the little boy in his arms and then shifted his gaze to the boy's mother. Something inside him turned over, and heat spilled through him. Not the fiery, lust-ridden flames that had been engulfing him for days. This was a warmth that seemed to slide into every dark and empty corner he possessed. Looking into her eyes gave him more than he'd had before. And even as he recognized that, he knew he couldn't keep it. Couldn't risk what he might find if he let his guard down.

Shaking his head, he asked, "Does it really matter?"

Disappointed by his evasion, she looked around her again, then rubbed her hands up and down her upper arms. "Griffin, you really shouldn't have done any of this."

Maybe not, but he wasn't sorry about it. "Yeah, well, I did."

"And now I have to pay you for it."

"Damn it, Nicole..."

"No," she said quickly. "It's the only way. I'll make...payments or something, I don't know. Shouldn't take more than twenty or thirty years," she added in a mutter.

He gave an audible sigh. The woman annoyed him as often as she intrigued him, and that was saying a hell of a lot. "Connor, your mother is the most stubborn woman in the world."

"That's pretty much pot-kettle territory," she pointed out.

Well, she had him there. "Fine. You want to pay me back? Do some work for my company."

He'd surprised her again.

"What? Now you want to hire me?"

He was out of options, Griffin told himself. If he wanted to make this right with her, and he did, then he had to do something. And work was the one thing Nicole completely understood. Her work ethic was as finely honed as his own, so he knew he had her with this one.

"You're not giving me much of a choice here, are you?"

"No." She lifted her chin. "I'm not. Okay, I'll work for you to pay off what you put into the kitchen, but I'm also going to pay you for the deductible."

"Damn it, Nicole," he said again and reached out to take her chin in his hand. "That's one thing we're not going to argue over. I started the fire, I'm paying the deductible. Deal with it."

Their gazes locked, tension hummed between them for several long seconds. Finally, though,

Nicole nodded. "Okay. You can pay the deductible, but I pay you back for every other expense you paid over the insurance money."

"Deal. I'm not happy, but it's a deal."

She took his fingers from her face and closed her hand around them. "It has to be this way, Griffin. We're not a couple. You don't owe me anything. We have to be able to deal with each other on even ground."

Even ground. Hell, he could buy and sell her a hundred times over. Financially, the cards were stacked in his favor. But he couldn't argue with her logic. They weren't a couple and weren't going to be one. What they had was temporary, and they'd both known that going in. It just fried him to be told he wasn't a part of her life, but he couldn't disagree, either. He nodded. "Even ground."

Nicole's nerves were jumping and tangled up with her anger and, okay, yes, excitement, was a deep sense of disappointment she couldn't shake. Griffin could color this any way he wanted to, but the truth was, he had done exactly what he wanted to do without a thought for how she might feel about it. An arrogant man with a generous streak. How was she supposed to stand against that combination?

She knew darn well that the King family stormed through life doing what they thought was best, and if that meant mowing someone down...well, they always felt bad about it later. Shaking her head, Nicole realized that she was just the latest in a long line of Griffin's conquests.

He was so used to women falling at his feet, no wonder he was confused over her reaction to his "gift." The man was both endearing and frustrating as all get-out. Somehow, he had remembered everything she'd told him about her dream kitchen. How had he found the perfect granite? The tiles she had seen only in her mind?

And her rooster. Her gaze flicked to the silly bird sitting on her new, truly fabulous stove. Griffin had cleaned the soot off the red teakettle until it, too, gleamed as if it was new.

Everything in Nicole wanted to go to him, but first she had to make him see *why* she was so upset about this.

"You went around me, Griffin."

"Yeah," he admitted, "I did."

"My ex used to do that, too," she said, reaching up to stroke her son's cheek. "He made my decisions for me because he thought I was too stupid to do it for myself."

"That's not what—"

She held up one hand for quiet. "Whether you meant it that way or not, that's how it feels."

He nodded slowly, as if finally understanding what she was thinking, feeling.

"If that's true, then…" He paused, took a breath and added, "I'm sorry."

Nicole smiled. "I think that's the first time I ever heard you say that."

One corner of his mouth quirked. "I don't say it often."

"Then thank you."

"You're welcome."

"Griff," Connor said, slapping one tiny hand against Griffin's cheek. "Wanna story now."

Instead of answering, Griffin looked at her. One dark eyebrow lifted. "Shall we go back?

Have dinner, read a story and get Connor ready for bed?"

"No bed," the boy wailed, flinging a wild glance at his mother.

"Maybe Connor and I should just stay here tonight."

"Kitchen's not completely finished yet," he said. "The crew will be in to check on grounding wires and that gas hookup for the stove tomorrow, so…"

So, Nicole thought, she could stay here and still not have a usable kitchen, or she could go back with Griffin and have one more night of the fantasy that had come to mean too much to her.

Not much of a contest.

"Okay then," she said. "Let's go back."

"Hear that, buddy?" Griffin asked as he headed for the doorway. "We're gonna go read a story."

"And no baf," Connor said solemnly.

Griffin was chuckling as Nicole paused on the threshold to look back at her dream kitchen. An involuntary sigh slipped from her throat. It was perfect.

And it was going to be a constant reminder of the man she had loved...and lost.

They made love that night in a room lit only by the pale light of the moon. Griffin looked into Nicole's eyes as he took her and felt the invisible threads between them tightening. The connection he felt with her was deepening, and he wasn't sure what the hell to do about it.

Leaving might not be enough this time, he told himself later as he lay awake and listened to Nicole's soft, steady breathing.

He was getting too attached. Too accustomed to being with Nicole and her son. Even when this time with her was over, he knew he'd carry her memory with him, and that hadn't been in the plan at all.

Still, leaving was his only recourse. He wouldn't risk the pain of loving and losing again. If that made him as big a coward as Lucas had turned out to be, then he'd just have to live with it. No sane man lined up for a sharp jab to the heart, so why the hell should he set himself up?

The only thing he could do was leave. Soon, he

assured himself as Nicole snuggled into him in the dark. He draped one arm around her and held her close even as his mind deliberately ignored the warning bells sounding out all around him.

Connor's voice warbled over the baby monitor. "Mommy?"

Griffin glanced down at Nicole. She was still sleeping, so he slipped out of bed, carefully disentangling himself so he wouldn't disturb her. Then in the dark, he walked across the hall to where Connor was awake and fretting.

The night-light threw a soft yellow light onto the ceiling, where it reflected and fell back down in a soft glow that illuminated the big bed and the tiny boy sitting up in the center of it. Connor wore blue, summer-weight, footie pajamas with baseball team logos stamped all over them. His blond hair was sticking straight up, and he clutched his alligator to his chest. His eyes widened when Griffin walked in.

"Me scared, Griff."

"Of what, buddy?" He kept his voice low and eased down to sit on the edge of the bed.

"Don't know." The little boy lay down, rubbed

his eyes with his fists, then grabbed hold of his alligator again.

"Well, don't be scared," Griffin told him, smoothing the boy's hair and speaking quietly. "I'll be right here, okay?"

"'Kay." Connor sighed and gave him a winsome smile that turned Griffin's insides to jelly. "You a good daddy."

While the little boy drifted back to sleep, Griffin sat there in the dimly lit darkness, stunned to his soul. A *daddy?* No. He looked at the child sleeping so innocently and took a huge mental leap backward. He couldn't do this. Couldn't risk this. He already felt too much for Connor and for Nicole. He couldn't let the boy believe that he was staying. That he would always be around to chase away the nightmares.

This whole thing had spiraled way out of control.

Time now to snap it back into line.

He walked back to his bedroom and stopped in the doorway. Nicole was sitting up in bed, watching him. Her blond hair was rumpled, and her lips were still puffy from his kiss. She looked, he thought, edible. His brain shouted out a clear warning even as other parts of him leaped to life.

"Is Connor okay?" she asked.

"Yeah, he went back to sleep." Griffin scrubbed both hands over his face and told himself to just say it. Get it out into the open. Get it over with.

"I heard what he said to you," Nicole told him softly and waved one hand toward the baby monitor on the bedside table.

He took a deep breath, nodded and said, "Good. Then I won't have to explain."

"Griffin…"

"Look, it's not fair to put Connor through this," he said, stalking toward the dresser and yanking open the drawers. As he tugged on a pair of jeans and a T-shirt, he looked over his shoulder at her and had to fight the urge to strip and get back in bed with her. More warning signs, when he was actually considering allowing his body to rule his mind. *Wasn't going to happen.*

"You're right." Nicole pulled the sheet and quilt up over her breasts, then let her hands fall into her lap. Swinging her hair out of her face, she gave him a smile that he didn't deserve. "We shouldn't have let it go on this long, Griffin."

"No, it's not that—" It was exactly that, but he didn't like hearing her say it. He tried to read her eyes, but the moonlight wasn't sharp enough to define the shadows he saw in those blue depths. Maybe that was for the best, he thought. Maybe he didn't want to know how she really felt, because then, leaving would be even harder.

"Connor's a little boy who wants a daddy," she said, lifting one shoulder in a casual shrug. "He's had fun with you. It's only natural he'd start to think of you in that way."

Didn't seem to be bothering her as much as it was bothering him, Griffin thought.

"I didn't mean to—"

"I know that, Griffin." She lifted one hand and tucked her hair behind her ear. "Just like I know you don't have to stage an escape from the house in the middle of the night. There's no reason for you to feel guilty."

He stopped what he was doing and realized she was right. An escape was exactly what he'd been trying for. And as much as he'd like to deny it, the only explanation was that he'd panicked, pure and simple. He'd wanted to go fast, to avoid hurting Nicole and Connor any more than he already had.

Hell, he'd wanted to avoid racking up more pain *himself*.

But there was no easy out here, he thought, gaze locked with Nicole's.

"Relax, Griffin," she said, a small, sad smile curving her mouth. "I'm not going to weep and wail and beg you not to go."

Why the hell not?

"We had our fling, and now it's over, right?"

He rested one hand on his chest and rubbed a throbbing ache there. It didn't help.

"Get some sleep, Griffin," she said. "We'll take care of the rest in the morning."

Ten

In the morning, he was gone.

Nicole found the note on top of a pillow and blanket Griffin had left stacked on the end of the couch where he'd slept after walking out of the room they had been sharing. The note was short and somewhat less than sweet.

I went into the office. Will be back this evening. If you need anything, call.

"If I need anything?" she whispered before crumpling the note in her hand. She bit down hard on her bottom lip to distract herself from the urge to cry again. *If she needed anything.* All she really needed was—no. Never mind.

She wouldn't go there again, not even in her own mind.

Nicole had spent most of the lonely night alternately crying and silently berating herself. *She* had done this. *She* had gone and fallen in love with a man who had run the moment things got complicated.

Her heart ached and her eyes burned from too little sleep and too many tears. Idiot. That's what she was. Because it wasn't only that she had allowed herself to fall in love with Griffin King, even knowing it wasn't safe. The worst part was that she had begun to *believe.*

Stupid, she knew, but that was what hurt the most. In spite of everything, even knowing that Griffin wasn't a forever kind of guy, Nicole had allowed herself to begin to believe in the fantasy of the two of them being together.

She ran one hand across the pillow he had used the night before, and then curled her fingers into her palm. She wasn't going to fall apart. Wasn't going to cry anymore, either. Because it wasn't only her pain she had to be concerned with now.

There was Connor to think about, and that's

what she was most furious about. Deluding herself into believing in a fantasy was one thing. She was a grown-up and would eventually get over the misery she'd brought down on her own head.

But Connor was just a baby. Not even three years old. When he loved, it was with his whole heart and he expected to be loved in return the same way. He was too young to know about betrayal or disappointment or what it was like for someone in your life to suddenly *not* be in it anymore.

At least Connor's father had left him before he was born. You couldn't miss something you'd never known. But Griffin was different.

She couldn't explain it to Connor; she could only hope that at some point, he'd forget about the man he'd loved enough to want for a daddy.

She hoped they would both forget.

But for the moment, the death of her dreams was raw and so painful, every breath drawn felt like a victory. She didn't have time to wallow, though.

So she went through the motions, getting her son up and dressed for the day. Then she carried Connor into the kitchen for breakfast. He whipped his head from side to side, looking around the empty room in confusion.

"Where Griff go?"

This was all her fault, she thought as she looked into her son's shining eyes. Her own pain she could handle, but knowing that her son would miss Griffin tore at her.

"Griffin had to go away, sweetie." She gave him some strawberries and a small cup of yogurt.

Connor banged his spoon on the chair tray. "Where? Connor go, too?"

"Not this time, baby," she soothed.

"Wanna go!"

His bottom lip quivered, and Nicole's heart twisted in her chest.

"We'll see," she said and silently cursed herself for using the stock parental phrase that usually translated into a big fat no.

Meanwhile, they'd get through breakfast, and once Connor was at preschool, Nicole would move their things back to their own house. Lucas would hurry up the finish work if she insisted, and she wasn't above using the threat of a lawsuit to make sure of it.

Once they were back where they belonged, she assured herself as she sipped at her coffee, she and Connor would both begin to heal.

A few days later, Nicole still hadn't seen Griffin, but her house was her own again and Katie and Rafe were back in town.

"I still think Rafe should beat him up," Katie said from her seat at Nicole's new kitchen table.

"And I appreciate the support," Nicole told her as she set a cup of coffee down in front of her best friend.

Connor was napping, the house was quiet and Nicole was still carrying around an icy ball of regret in the center of her chest. But true to her vow, she hadn't cried since the night Griffin had walked away from her. It had been close a time or two, but she'd sucked it up and swallowed the pain, forcing it down into a corner of her heart, where it continued to simmer and churn.

"We've talked about this a dozen times since you got home," Nicole reminded her friend.

"And I'm still frustrated because you won't let me sic Rafe on Griffin. Trust me," Katie said, "he'd be happy to help."

Nicole laughed a little and braced both elbows on the tabletop. "I bet. He's probably been getting an earful from you every day."

Katie smiled and shrugged. "He has. Hey, that's the husband's job. To listen when his wife needs to rant about a scum-sucking, no-good, lying rat of a man who hurt her best friend."

Nicole sighed and reached for one of the dark chocolate raspberry cookies Katie had brought with her. She took a bite and barely noticed the amazing flavors exploding on her tongue.

"Again," she said, "appreciate the support, but Griffin didn't do this to me. I did."

"Bull."

Shaking her head, Nicole said, "He never once pretended that what we had was anything but temporary." Hard to say it out loud, but maybe she needed to hear it all again, too. "I'm the one who built fantasies in the air. I'm the one who fell in love. It's my own damn fault, Katie. You can't blame Griffin for it, as much as I'd like to."

Katie sighed and snatched up a cookie. Taking a huge bite and chewing as if she were biting through steel chips, she asked, "How's Connor dealing?"

Here was where the guilt rolled in.

"He still asks for Griffin. Wants to go see him. And wakes up at night crying for him." Which pretty much described how Nicole was feeling, too. Except for the crying. She wouldn't cry. She refused to spend one more tear on the man she'd loved and lost.

Katie dropped one hand to the slight swell of her belly. "I'm so sorry this all turned out so badly. I hate knowing Connor's so upset."

"Me, too," Nicole said softly. "But it's getting better." And maybe if she said that often enough, it would even be true eventually.

"Well." Katie looked around the redone kitchen and said, "Even though they sneaked this in on you, I have to say King Construction really does nice work. The kitchen's gorgeous."

"It really is." Nicole's gaze swept the room. "I know I should still be furious at Griffin for wangling all of this, but I do love the kitchen. It's exactly as I always imagined it."

And every time she stepped into the room, she remembered the man who had arranged it for her. Nicole wondered how long that would last. How long would his memory be stamped on her house? Her heart? Depressingly enough, she figured it would be only a day or two short of forever.

Needing a change of subject desperately, Nicole said, "You still haven't told me about Italy."

Katie looked at her, reached across the table to take her hand and smiled as she squeezed briefly. "Right. Okay then, let me tell you about Tuscany…"

As Katie talked, Nicole pushed thoughts of Griffin aside and concentrated solely on her friend's voice. With a little effort, she told herself firmly, every day would get better. And soon, Griffin would no longer be front and center in her mind.

She hoped.

* * *

"Janice," Griffin snapped into the phone, "when Garrett calls, put him right through."

"I always do," she replied, and he heard the stiffness in her voice.

No surprise there. His assistant hadn't been happy when he ended his vacation early. Especially since he'd returned in a mood that made Jack the Ripper look congenial.

"Fine," he said, scraping one hand across his face, "just…bring me the plan for the museum job."

"Right away." She hung up, and Griffin set the phone back in its cradle with a deliberate softness.

If he hadn't, he might have been tempted to throw the damn thing across the room. He felt like a man on the edge all the time now.

"Probably because you're not sleeping," he muttered. When he left Rafe and Katie's house, he'd moved straight into a hotel. He hadn't been able to stay there, right next door to Nicole and Connor. Not without going to see them, and that wouldn't have helped a damn thing.

So for three days now, he'd spent most of his time at the office, and when exhaustion forced him to leave, he went to the penthouse suite at the Beachside. There he sat out on the balcony, stared into the darkness and wished he was with Nicole.

For all the good that did him.

There was no going back.

He leaned deeper into his chair and glanced around the interior of his office. It was practically a duplicate of his twin's. He and Garrett had adjoining offices, with a bathroom, complete with shower, separating the rooms. A lot of times he'd found himself working around the clock and being damned grateful for a shower and a change of clothes here at the office.

Plush, burgundy-leather furniture dotted the room. Framed family photos took up most of one wall. On the opposite wall was a flat-screen TV, dark now, and a few awards King Security had been given over the course of the years. There was also a wet bar for entertaining clients. Back in the day, he and Garrett would be shouting back and forth between their offices, laughing, talking about the job.

But Garrett was with his wife, and all Griffin had was an overdose of silence.

His business was in great shape. It was only his life that sucked at the moment.

But that could change. All he had to do was pick up the phone and make a call. He could lose himself on a succession of dates at five-star restaurants with gorgeous women. He could reclaim the life he knew and let go of the whole maturity thing.

"Mature's overrated anyway," he muttered. "Let Garrett and the others do the one-woman thing. Somebody's gotta pick up the slack."

He actually reached for the phone before he stopped and let his hand fall to his desk. He wasn't interested in a date. Hell, he wasn't even interested in finding a new home, now that his Realtor had sold his condo.

Nothing interested him, and that was the truth.

Not a new house. Not a job. Nothing.

Which only fed the frustration and anger swimming through him.

His office door flew open and crashed into the wall behind it. Griffin jumped to his feet and faced his cousin.

"Rafe, what the hell?"

Rafe King stood in the doorway, feet braced and hands curled into fists. "I want to know why you screwed everything up so badly that all my wife does is tell me to kick your ass."

Griffin looked past his cousin at Janice. His assistant stood by, shaking her head, without the slightest hint of surprise on her face. That came, he supposed, with experience working with the King family. Tempers were fast and volatile and usually drained away just as quickly.

As for Griffin, he wasn't surprised to see his cousin, either. Hell, he'd been expecting Rafe for days now. Might as well get it over with.

"At least close the damn door."

Rafe did, then turned back to him. "What the hell, dude? Nicole? You had to go there? *Really?*"

Rafe's temper had already eased back enough that punching didn't seem to be on the menu. A shame, really. Griffin could have used a good fight to blow off steam. Instead, still irritated, still frustrated, Griffin came around his desk and leaned back to sit on the edge. "Didn't plan it that way."

"Well, of course not," Rafe said, perching beside him. "Clearly there was no plan at all. Would've been good, though."

"Yeah, would've." Griffin glanced at his cousin. "Tell you the truth? Don't know what the hell I was thinking."

"Yeah, I know how that feels," Rafe admitted. "The minute I met Katie, I couldn't think of anything but—" He stopped and shrugged. "You know."

"All too well," Griffin admitted, then asked, "Did Lucas tell you the story of Nicole's kitchen?"

"He did." Rafe frowned. "Moron's lucky Nicole didn't sue him. Us." He shook his head. "You can't just ignore a customer's signed contract, you know?"

"Wasn't his idea," Griffin told him and felt a twinge of guilt for the crap Lucas had no doubt been getting from Rafe. "That's on me, too."

His cousin snorted a laugh. "Busy couple weeks for you, wasn't it?"

"You could say that." Griffin shook his head, too. Hell, the last couple of weeks were sort of a blur. He'd been so far off his normal stride, he was stumbling now, trying to get back to it. At least that was what he told himself. It wasn't, he assured himself, that he didn't *want* to go back to the way things were.

Of course he did. What he was feeling now was residual lust, that's all. He'd get over it. He *always* got over the current woman in his life when he was ready to move on. And he was ready, damn it.

First, though, he had to deal with his cousin and whatever family crap was going to rain down on him. "So," he asked, "you come to fight?"

"That was my original thought," Rafe said as he folded his arms over his chest. "But I'm over it." He looked at Griffin. "The question is, are you?"

"Am I what?"

"Over it. Nicole, I mean."

"I will be." He sounded certain. Too bad he wasn't feeling it.

"Yeah," Rafe said with a chuckle. "Keep telling yourself that."

"Y'know," Griffin pointed out, "the way you almost screwed up your chance with Katie doesn't exactly make you the big relationship expert of the family."

"Key word there being *almost*," Rafe said and stood up. "I'm not going to give you advice. Hell, you wouldn't listen even if I did."

"True."

"I am going to tell you if you walk away you'll be kicking yourself for the rest of your life."

Griffin's head snapped up and he fixed a narrowed gaze on his cousin. "Stay out of this, Rafe. Seriously."

He held up both hands. "Oh, I'm out. Trust me. You're on your own here."

"Good." Annoyance flared to life inside him, and Griffin stood up, too.

"Now, I'm going home to have some of the dark chocolate and meringue cookies Katie was making when I left." He grinned. "Which you, by the way, will never taste."

"Bastard."

"Damn straight." Whistling, Rafe left the office, and as he went out, Janice scuttled in, carrying a manila file folder.

"Here are the details on the museum job."

"Thanks," Griffin muttered and snatched the file from her. She left a moment later, and Griffin was alone again.

He really hated being alone.

He left work early.

No point in being there if he couldn't damn well *think*. Instead, he went to the beach. Yeah, he hated crowds, but lately he'd discovered he hated being alone more.

The sea wind rushed at him as he walked along the ocean's edge, bare feet just brushing past the lacy slide of the water onto the sand. The sun was hot, the sand damp and chill, and the sounds and smells around him invaded in a rush.

He saw a couple of kids playing in the sand and remembered making castles for Connor to knock down. He caught the scent of hot dogs on a grill and remembered barbecues in the backyard. He determinedly walked past a young couple so wrapped up in the kiss enveloping them, they were oblivious to everyone else. And he remembered kissing Nicole.

Remembered the taste of her, the scent of her, the soft sigh of her breath on his neck when she leaned into him. He remembered how she felt in his arms and how empty those same arms felt now that she was out of his life.

Griffin pushed one hand through his hair and muttered, "This isn't working. None of it is."

She was burned into his brain, his heart.

"What the hell am I supposed to do with this?" he demanded of no one.

Someone shrieked, and Griffin whipped around to watch a woman get tossed into the water by her boyfriend. Laughter pealed out and he gritted his teeth against the envy that washed over him.

He didn't think about it, just acted. Pulling his phone from his pocket, he dialed a number and waited. When she answered, the mere sound of her voice lit up his insides.

"Nicole?"

There was a long pause. "Griffin. Hi."

Well, she could have sounded less enthusiastic. If he'd offered her a bouquet of poison ivy. Had he really expected her to greet him with nothing but welcome? Hell, he was lucky she hadn't hung up yet. Calling her was a bad idea, he told himself, but he couldn't regret it. Turning, he stared out at the sunlight glinting on the surface of the water.

They'd made a deal, right? That she would work for his company. So he had a right to call her to talk details. That's all this was. Business.

"Yeah. I wanted to know if you were serious about working off the deductible on the kitchen."

Another long pause. Hell, this was tough on a man's pride.

"Of course I was. I told you I don't need you to buy things for me."

"Yeah," he said, cutting her off as a kid raced by, splashing water into the breezy air. "I remember. So the deal is, we've got the museum security job coming up and since you're already familiar with the proposal, I thought you could start with that. Work out the numbers on payroll for the guards, say, in four- and six-hour shifts."

"Fine."

He imagined her sitting in her new kitchen in a

splash of sunlight, her eyes narrowed in thought. Maybe Connor was in the room, too, playing at her feet. Then he pushed those images aside and focused on the matter at hand.

"How's Connor?" he blurted.

"Connor's fine," she said tightly, and he could hear the tension in her voice. "I'm fine."

"Good to hear." What the hell else could he say? He's the one who had opened up this chasm between them. But in his defense, he thought wildly, splitting up had been their deal all along. So he pushed aside regrets. "Okay then. I'll have Janice overnight you the plans and you can get to work."

He was good at thinking on his feet, he silently commended himself. He'd only come up with this idea a few minutes ago and it was spilling from him like he'd been working it out for days. "I'll need a complete write-up on the expenses by the end of the week."

"You'll have it," she said firmly. "Is that it?"

No, he thought. There was more. There was admitting that he couldn't sleep without her curled up beside him. That he woke up craving the taste of her more than his first cup of coffee. That breathing was disappointing because her peach scent didn't flavor every breath.

But that would make him pretty damn pathetic, wouldn't it?

"Yeah. That's it."

"Okay then," she said. "Goodbye, Griffin."

She hung up, and Griffin just managed to keep from tossing his phone into the sea.

Sunlight filled her gorgeous new kitchen and still Nicole felt as if she was at the bottom of a very black hole.

Griffin's voice had caught her off guard. She hadn't been prepared for it. Hadn't been able to steel herself against the pain that ripped into her like the slash of a knife. Days now, she'd been working at getting over Griffin. She'd concentrated on her work and her son and had almost convinced herself that her life was normal again.

Then he had to call.

She stared at her cell phone and willed the misery she felt into a small, dark corner of her heart.

She wouldn't give in to it, because once she did, she didn't think she'd be able to stop.

"Griff coming?" Connor's voice steadied her.

She had to hold it together, if not for her, then for her son's sake.

"No, sweetie, Griff's not coming today."

"Tomorrow?"

Nicole scooped him up into her arms and held him close. Inhaling the soft, sweet scent of him, she heard herself say, "We'll see…"

Eleven

Life in a palace had its perks.

Solitude wasn't one of them.

Griffin had never seen so many people. Which worked well enough for him at the moment, but he just couldn't figure out how Garrett managed to put up with it every day. There were dozens of servants working around the palace.

Maids, chefs, gardeners, footmen…*footmen,* for God's sake. He guessed that living in a castle meant you were predisposed to embracing the Middle Ages.

Coming to Cadria to see his twin had been a spur-of-the-moment decision. That's where being a member of the King family came with its own perks—all he had to do was make a call and suddenly one of the family's jets was at his disposal. Beat the hell out of security lines and hassles at the airport.

He stepped up and braced one boot on the bottom rung of a pristinely painted white fence and stared out across grounds so tidy it was as if they'd been manicured with scissors. The sun was out and huge white clouds sailed across a sky blue enough to make your eyes ache if you stared at it for too long. Ancient trees stood like soldiers around the perimeter of the fence, dropping shade from twisted, gnarled limbs.

The wind tousled his hair, and behind his dark glasses, Griffin squinted into the distance. The palace grounds were immense and as pretty as a painting. There was a massive stable adjoining the paddock that was as big as Nicole's neighborhood. Behind him, closer to the palace, was a hedge maze and a rose garden that filled the air with amazing scents.

Despite the fact that Griffin wasn't a big fan of horses, he felt more comfortable out here than he did inside the castle. There was too much protocol there. Too much formality. Out here, there was too much time to think—but given a choice...

"Since when do you like horses?"

Griffin didn't even turn around. His arms were crossed on the top bar of the fence as he watched million-dollar horses being put through their paces by their trainers.

"I don't. They're big, and they have mean eyes." He laughed. "They're okay to watch—from a distance—never could understand riding them." He finally glanced at his twin. "That's your thing."

Garrett had always loved going riding, the one thing as twins that they'd never shared.

"Yeah," Garrett mused, taking up his brother's pose at the fence. "Have to admit, it's great to be able to come out here and ride whenever I want to."

"So being royal doesn't suck."

"Not even a little," Garrett told him on a half laugh.

"Good for you." Griffin really was glad his brother was happy. He just wished he himself wasn't so...hell, he didn't even know what he was.

"So what's going on?" Garrett turned his head and stared at Griffin. "Not that I'm not glad to see you any time, but you've got a job in L.A. to see to and you were just here a couple months ago."

Griffin squinted even tighter. Not that he was interested in the view, but it was better than meeting his twin's too-sharp gaze. Seeing Garrett and his wife, Alexis, so happy together made Griffin almost sorry he'd come to Cadria. Hell, how could Garrett understand where Griffin was coming from when he was locked into his own little fantasy world, here in the palace?

"It's Nicole, isn't it?" Garrett stared hard at him until Griffin turned his head to meet his eyes.

"What're you, psychic?"

"Yeah, like it takes a psychic to figure out what's eating at you." Garrett laughed a little and looked back out at the horses.

Well, hell. That's why he'd come here, wasn't it? Because no one knew him like his twin did. "Fine. Great. One look at me, and you can see I'm miserable. Nice to know that gives you a lift."

"I'm only laughing because it wasn't so long

ago that you were giving me the same kind of advice that I'm about to give you."

"Even better. Secondhand advice. That'll help." Disgusted, Griffin scowled at his twin.

"Hey, you're the one who came to me, remember?"

"Shows you just how bad off I am," he muttered.

"Yeah, good to see," Garrett said, slapping his twin on the back.

"Thanks very much," Griffin muttered.

"I was worried when you started up with Nicole," Garrett admitted. "She's not the kind of woman to use and then dump."

"I didn't dump her," Griffin argued. No, he hadn't. He'd damn well panicked and run for it.

That was still eating at him.

"You didn't do anything to keep her, either, did you?"

No, he hadn't, Griffin thought, and wondered if it was possible to kick himself. If not, he was pretty sure Garrett would gladly do it for him.

"So now you're the expert on women, is that it?" Griffin laughed shortly.

"No," Garrett admitted with a smile, "but I'm an expert on you."

He snorted. "Please."

"Not only are we twins," Garrett went on as if his brother hadn't spoken, "but we're both Kings."

"And that means?"

"It means we'll stick to our guns even if they end up turning on us." Garrett frowned and looked out over the paddock. His voice dropped, became thoughtful. "The trainers here, they work with a stallion and they sort of sneak up on him."

"Seriously?" Griffin just stared at his twin. "You're gonna give me horse talk?"

"The reason why is," Garrett continued, "the stallion doesn't even know it's happening, but slowly, old habits are broken. New ones are born. And pretty soon, the damn horse figures everything he's doing is all his idea."

"Right. Thanks. That's clear."

"It would be if your head wasn't so far up your—" He took a breath, worked his jaw for a second or two then tried again. "The problem is, this thing with Nicole jumped up on you from out of nowhere, so your first instinct is to fight it, even if it's what you want."

"Who says it's what I want?" Griffin mumbled.

"You do," Garrett shot back. "Just by being here, you're telling me that you're miserable without her."

"I don't remember saying that."

"Like you would," Garrett said on a snort. "Remember the night you gave me hell about Alexis?"

Griffin scowled. "Vaguely."

Another snort. "Then let me remind you. You told me I was a moron for standing back instead of going after what I want. Well, happy to tell you the same damn thing."

"Excuse me?"

"Who the hell else can call you that without expecting a fist to the face, if it's not your twin?"

"Don't count on the twin thing saving your ass."

"I can still take you."

"Not on your best day," Griffin assured him and asked himself why the hell he'd come to Cadria in the first place. He should have known it would go like this, Garrett-the-know-it-all pontificating from the mount of his happiness.

As for what he'd said, this was nothing like the situation his brother had been in with Alex. There had been lies separating them. Lies Garrett had told and Alex had caught him in.

This was different.

"The problem here is," Garrett was saying, as a cool breeze slipped past them, "that you're used to dealing with the temporary kind of woman. What did you used to say? 'Dating a woman with more than two brain cells is a waste of time'?"

Griffin gave him a tight grimace that couldn't have been mistaken for a smile.

"So what's your deal?" his twin asked. "You want to go back to spending time with women who talk about exfoliating and how to make their skin…what did you call it? *Shimmery?*"

Griffin groaned and closed his eyes. Yeah, he remembered saying all of that to Garrett. He remembered all of the nights spent being bored to tears just to be able to take a woman to his bed for a couple of hours.

"You told me once that I lived more in King

Jets than I did at my condo," Garrett said softly. "You were right. But the thing is, you don't even have that. Your condo's sold. You're killing time in a hotel. Damn it, Griff, where is the place you've felt most at home?"

He sighed and gave up fighting the truth. "With Nicole."

Nodding, Garrett accepted his twin's surrender and added, "Not only is she making you nuts, but she's smarter than both of us."

"What?"

Garrett grinned. "She noticed the significance of that ugly-ass brooch in the gem collection. Neither one of us did."

"I would have, eventually," Griffin said.

"That's the thing," Garrett told him. "You didn't have to, because she did. That's what being a team is, Griff. And if you're as smart as you're always telling me you are, you won't let her get away."

Griffin's heart told him Garrett was right. But his mind was still struggling. "How can I do that again? Nicole's a package deal. There's Connor to think about, too."

"And you're remembering Jamie."

"Yeah." Griffin turned to look at his twin. "Having that kid torn out of my life was hard."

"I know it was," Garrett said and slapped his brother on the back. "The difference this time is that Nicole didn't take Connor away. You *walked* away. From both of them."

That truth hit him hard. To protect himself from losing what was important to him—Nicole and Connor—he'd turned his back on them.

In the paddock one of the prized stallions suddenly erupted into a wild gallop, hooves churning the soft earth, mane flying.

"God, I'm an idiot."

"Congratulations," Garrett said with a chuckle. "It's hard to admit, but once you do, you can fix things."

"I don't know," Griffin told him, his heart still heavy, his mind racing with possibilities. "I think I might have blown any chance I had there. I not only walked out on Nicole, but on her son. No way is she going to forgive me for *that*. Her ex-husband did the same damn thing to her before Connor was even born."

"Useless male," Garrett muttered.

Griffin agreed. And it shamed him to realize that he'd walked out on them, too.

"He never went back. You will," Garrett said firmly, catching his brother's attention. "You make a mistake, you fix it. It's the King way. Hell, it's *your* way. In spite of what I usually tell you, you're not an idiot, Griffin. You know what you want. You knew when you came here. You just wanted to hear me say it out loud."

His twin was right, damn it. Griffin hadn't had one easy moment since he'd left Nicole. He had to try to get her back. Damned if he was going to lose the best thing he'd ever found.

"Hell," he said wryly, imagining the look on Nicole's face when he showed up at her house, "she'll probably slam the door in my face."

"You won't know until you try."

Shaking his head, Griffin argued, "Nicole and Connor both deserve the best. What if I suck at being a husband and an instant father? Is it fair to them to risk it?"

"Griffin, you've never sucked at a damn thing if you wanted it badly enough." Garrett reached over and gave his twin's shoulder a hard shove. "If they deserve the best, then give it to them."

Griffin nodded, feeling his old self-confidence come rushing back. He'd been second-guessing himself when it came to Nicole for so long, it was a relief to finally see his path laid out in front of him. Hell, yes, they deserved the best. And he'd damn well make sure they got it.

"So?" Garrett asked. "You going to be at the palace for dinner tonight?"

Griffin grinned. "Hell, no, I'm going home. To Nicole."

Nicole missed Griffin so much, it was a physical ache.

It had been days and nothing had changed. If anything, the pain kept growing, swelling inside her until she could hardly breathe. But it wasn't only her pain she had to deal with.

Connor had been moping around in toddler misery. Every day he asked for Griffin and every day, she explained that Griffin had had to go away. Her son's pain layered over hers until Nicole felt as though she was drowning.

Middle-of-the-night television was less than thrilling, but it beat lying in bed, trying futilely for sleep. She sat on the couch in her tank top and boxer-short PJs, flipping mindlessly through the channels until she came to an infomercial about psychics. For only five dollars a minute, you could have a stranger tell you how to fix your life.

But she didn't need a psychic for that. What she needed was what she'd already lost.

Outside, the world was quiet, peaceful. Inside, the television sound was set to whisper. So when the doorbell rang, she jumped a foot off the couch and then hurried to the front door. She grabbed the phone on the way, just in case she needed to call 911. But then, what kind of mad-dog burglar would ring the bell?

She looked out the window at the front porch and her heart jolted hard into life when she saw Griffin standing there in the soft glow of the porch light.

Why was he here? What should she do? Ignore him? Open the door just so she could slam it?

He rang the bell again, and her decision was

made. If Griffin kept that up, Connor would wake, and then she'd spend a half hour getting her son back to sleep.

Flipping the locks, she opened the door and looked up into blue eyes that locked on her like twin lasers. "Griffin, what do you want?"

"You."

"What?" Impossible. She was dreaming again. It was the only explanation. In the snatches of sleep she'd managed to grab over the last few days, her mind had tortured her with dreams just like this one, dreams in which Griffin came back, begged her forgiveness—like a King would ever do that—and pledged his undying love. The dreams always ended the same way, too—with Nicole waking up, emptier than when she'd fallen asleep.

He slapped one hand to the door as if to prevent her from closing it. "Can I come in?"

So, then, no dream.

"I don't think so," she said, though it cost her. What she wanted was to throw herself into his arms and feel him hold her close again. She wanted to *feel*. To come out of this half-waking life she'd been living.

But at the heart of all of this, in spite of her wants and needs and wishes and dreams, lay one truth. Griffin hadn't just walked away from *her*. He'd walked out on Connor. He'd broken her son's heart, and she didn't think she could forgive him for that.

"Okay," he said quickly, "I can understand that. You're pissed. You've got a right to be."

"It's way beyond pissed, Griffin," she told him and felt her spine snap into place. "You disappeared. Connor's been asking for you every day, and all I can tell him is that you had to go away."

His jaw clenched, and he let his head fall back for a moment. "I know. And I'm sorry."

"I heard you, you know," she said, deliberately keeping her gaze locked on his. "That day on the beach when you told your brother you felt sorry for Connor. Well, he doesn't need your pity. And neither do I."

His head dropped to his chest before he looked at her again. "That was bull. I never felt sorry for Connor. Why the hell would I? He has every-thing. He has *you*."

One small hurt washed away with his words. But it wasn't enough yet.

"I'm sorry, Nicole. For so damn much."

"I'm not the one you need to say that to. Well," she corrected, "not the only one."

"I know that, too," he told her, meeting her gaze again. "The reason I came here now, in the mid-dle of the night, was to make sure Connor was asleep. So if you tell me to go away, I will, and he'll never have to know I was here."

She flinched.

"But don't tell me to go away," he added quickly.

"Why shouldn't I?" she asked warily.

He bent down to retrieve a large white bag that sat at his feet. She hadn't noticed it before. No surprise, since she hadn't been able to take her eyes off him.

Reaching into the bag, he pulled out a small, green velvet box.

Nicole's heart actually stopped. She slapped one hand to her chest as if to get it beating again.

If this was a dream, she really didn't want to wake up this time.

Opening the box, he showed her the ring inside. "A star sapphire," he said. "Because it reminds me of your eyes. A deep, rich blue, but with stars and secrets hidden in their depths."

"Griffin…" Shaking her head, she looked from the beautiful ring to his face, to his eyes, and what she saw there stole her breath.

This was way better than her dreams, Nicole thought. The promise, the love, the future she saw in his expression was more than her mind could ever have conjured.

"There's more," he said before she could say anything else. He dipped into the bag again and pulled out a fireman's hat. "It's for Connor," he said unnecessarily. "He really loved sitting on that fire truck, so I thought…"

She reached out and took the hat from him, running her hands over the slick, plastic brim. It was bright red, with a shiny gold plastic badge, and Connor would love it. Tears filled her eyes as she looked up at the man watching her so stoically.

"Please let me in, Nicole," he whispered.

How could she not? Even if she only wanted to cling to her anger and hurt, she would have been moved by this late-night visit. But she wanted so much more than to stay mired in pain.

Nodding, she stepped back, and once he was in the house, he closed the door, sealing them into the room together. He took the fire hat from her and set it down onto the nearest table.

The room was dark, lit only by the television and from the streetlights outside. Still clutching the ring box in one hand, Griffin reached out and used his free hand to stroke her cheek. The feel of his skin against hers again was magic, Nicole thought, and she fervently hoped that there was a forever here they could both grab hold of.

But first, she had to hear him out. Had to be sure that he'd never leave again. She could risk her own heart, but she wouldn't put her son's happiness on the line.

"I was wrong, Nicole," he whispered. "I never should have left. Never should have risked losing you forever. My only excuse is, I hadn't planned on falling in love. You caught me off guard."

"You did the same to me," she said.

"See, I never actually thought I was capable of the kind of love I feel for you. I never saw myself getting married or being a father—"

She pulled back instinctively, but he held on to her.

"That was then. This is now. I love you, Nicole. I love Connor. I want us to get married," he told her. "I want to adopt Connor, if you'll let me. I want to be your husband and his father. I want more kids. As many as we can have," he said, warming to his theme, a smile curving his mouth. "Nothing the Kings like better than big families."

"More kids."

"Lots of 'em." He swore it, his voice carrying the ring of truth, of desire.

For the first time that night, tears filmed her eyes and spilled over. Griffin reacted instantly, moving in to sweep the tears aside with his thumb and then pull her into him, nestling her body against his. "I swear to you, that's the last time I will ever make you cry, Nicole. No more tears."

She wanted so desperately to believe. To let

herself grab this happiness and hold on to it. For her and for Connor.

"I'm asking you for a chance, Nicole," he said, leaning back until their eyes could meet and hold. "One more chance to prove how much I love you both. To show you that I'm the only man in the world for you." He bent down and kissed her mouth quickly, firmly. "I swear I'm worth the trouble."

She laughed a little, and it felt as if the ice around her heart was shattering.

"I'm taking that as a good sign," he said, giving her a half smile that tugged at her heart and soul. "But I want you to know, even if you say no to me tonight, I'm not going away. Not ever. I know what I want now, Nicole. And I'm willing to fight for it. I'll wait for you to be sure. But I won't give up. Not on you. Not on us."

He caught her chin in his fingers and rubbed her skin with his thumb. "I'll come back tomorrow night and the night after that and the night after that until I finally convince you."

"You think you can?" she asked, loving this side of him. Loving being with him again and feeling the hope for a shiny future rising up inside her.

"Honey, I'm a King. There's nothing we can't do," he assured her.

"Griff?" Connor walked into the room and both adults turned to the little boy in his sleeper jammies. Clutching his alligator in the crook of one arm, the child looked up at Griffin and gave him a huge grin. "Griff is back!"

"Yeah, buddy," he said, giving Nicole a cautious glance. "I'm back. I promise I won't go away again."

Connor raced to him, and Griffin swung the boy up into his arms.

"Connor missed you," the boy said solemnly.

"I know, and I'm sorry," Griffin told him. "I missed you, too. But I brought you a present." He reached for the hat, plunked it down onto the boy's head and grinned at him.

"Fireman!" Connor shouted with glee.

Nicole's heart couldn't be fuller. She watched her son and the man she loved together and her whole world suddenly fell into place. Everything was just as it should be. All she had to do was take a single leap of faith. To trust in the love she felt and the love she could see in Griffin's eyes.

"Mommy, Griff is back!"

"I see that," she said, moving in closer to the two men in her life. "I think he should stay, don't you?"

Griffin's gaze locked on hers. His heart was in his eyes, and she read everything she needed to know right there. This wasn't a gamble. This was the best thing that had ever happened to her. And she wasn't going to miss a minute of it.

"Stay!" Connor blurted, then leaned into Griffin. "And a story."

"You bet, little guy," Griffin said and held out the beautiful sapphire-and-gold ring toward Nicole.

She lifted her left hand and watched as he slid the ring onto her finger. Its weight was perfect. Everything was perfect.

In the flickering light of the television, a family was made.

Nicole leaned into Griffin and felt his arm come around her. Here was her dream come true. Here was everything she would ever need.

"Let's put our son to bed," Griffin said with a smile, "then we can...*talk*. I'll prove to you just how much I missed you."

Love flared into life inside her and washed through her with a wave strong enough to wipe away disappointments and hurts and everything but the rightness of this moment.

There was only one thing left to say to him.

"Welcome home, Griffin."

* * * * *